What Legends Are Made Of

A Paranormal Romance Anthology

by

Heather Beck

DIAMOND DUST BOOKS

What Legends Are Made Of
ISBN: 978-1-926990-00-2
Copyright © 2011 Heather Beck
Cover Photo Copyright © Konrad Bak/Fotolia

Published by
Diamond Dust Books

Prologue

Have you ever experienced a story filled with so much suspense, terror and romance that you couldn't get it out of your mind? Be prepared to feel all of these emotions because I'm about to take you on a journey that you won't soon forget.

You're personally invited to tour the halls of Sir Tristan's Estate, a place where ghosts roam freely and enter your dreams at night. Following your stay at the estate, you'll cruise on the Blue Oceana, a perfect ship for sightseeing. With patience and a careful eye you might see the merman that lives in the crystal clear ocean. If you enjoyed watching the odd ocean creature while aboard the ship, you'll love Frank Stanford's Freak Show. There you'll see a unicorn with wings and a talking tree. However, it's the freak show's horrifying main attraction that shocks everyone who sees it. If you can stop shaking after your encounter with freaky Frank, continue to Karyn and Max Shield's Costume and Magic Shop; just be careful of what you purchase there since the merchandise is perhaps too realistic.

Some stories make your heart soar, while others make you scream aloud; these stories will make you do both. They'll leave you spellbound and yearning for more. Ready to find out what real legends are made of? Turn the page...

Table Of Contents:

Sir Tristan's Estate

Twenty-year-old Skye Huntington gazed out the airplane's window as it descended towards the ground. Her view of the tree covered hills was obscured by the settling dusk. She turned her eyes towards the brightly lit runway and watched as the neon orange line simultaneously grew closer and lost momentum.

Skye grasped the sides of her chair as the airplane shook. To supercede her nervousness, she thought about the reason for her trip.

She was assigned to capture the sadness behind the Sir Tristan Estate. Honored that the editor of America's Amazing Architectures Magazine would choose a photographer who had only been working professionally for a year, Skye enthusiastically accepted the assignment. She knew very little about the estate; however, what she did know intrigued her.

The estate was built in the late eighteenth century by the Tristans. It had ten acres of cotton fields, worked by slaves. The decline of the estate was partly due to the loss of the slaves, which occurred before the civil war and President Lincoln's declaration of human rights. Since Sir Tristan was responsible for freeing the slaves, the government of Virginia honored him by renaming the estate. The government's decision to do so wasn't a difficult one. Sir Tristan was a martyr with ambitions to free all the slaves of the South and gain equality for women. Although he achieved many of his goals, they came with a price – his happiness.

Sir Tristan, an only child, died alone at the estate on October 28, 1860. He was unmarried and left no heirs. After his death, the estate became the property of the government, who turned it into a profitable tourist attraction and bed and breakfast one hundred years later.

That was the extent of Skye's knowledge of the estate. Perhaps that's why the editor of America's Amazing Architectures Magazine had requested the presence of a historical interpreter.

Skye watched as the conveyer belt turned round and round. Her eyes scanned the surplus of luggage until the familiar dark green suitcase appeared. She grabbed the suitcase before it could make its second trip around the belt. Although her eyes were alert, her mind was foggy.

She whistled down a taxi and watched as the driver exited the vehicle to help her put the luggage into the trunk.

"Thank you."

"My pleasure," the taxi driver, who was a young man of about twenty five years, replied. "Where to?"

"The Sir Tristan Estate, please."

The driver turned to cast Skye a curious glance. "Excuse me, miss?"

"The - Sir - Tristan - Estate," Skye repeated slowly.

"Are you sure you want to go *there*?"

"Of course." Skye was annoyed at the driver's uncertainty. "Is there any reason why I wouldn't want to go to the estate?"

"Yes."

Skye looked at the roof of the taxi, as if seeking unknown help. "And why is that?"

"It's been closed for a week."

Skye's eyes widened in surprise. "That's not possible. I'm here on business. My boss has made arrangements for me to photograph the Sir Tristan Estate."

"Oh," the driver muttered, turning in his seat. "I guess they made an exception for you."

Skye settled back in her seat, glad they were finally on their way, but confused about her situation. "Why have they closed the estate to the public?"

"It's a pretty amazing story," the driver replied, glancing at Skye quickly in his rearview mirror. "During an independent tour with his family, a ten-year-old boy discovered an old document in a desk which presumably belonged to Sir Tristan. The boy didn't inform his parents about the discovery; instead, he placed it up his t-shirt and tried to exit the estate with it. However, as he was leaving, the document slipped out from under his t-shirt. The boy's parents, who thought he had stolen it from the gift shop, scolded and lectured him. Meanwhile, the woman at the exit was in shock. Being a fifteen year employee of the estate, she was flabbergasted at the boy's find. She knew it wasn't a fake; it was a real document containing unknown knowledge."

"Really?" Skye leaned forward. "What kind of document?"

"It was a birth certificate."

"Whose?"

"Miss Kathleen Tristan."

Skye looked at the driver's reflection in the rear-view mirror. Her mind raced as she tried to fit together the broken pieces. "Who was Miss Kathleen Tristan?"

"No one knows."

Then I shouldn't feel so bad for not being able to figure it out either, Skye thought. "You haven't explained why the Sir Tristan Estate has been closed for tourism," she reminded.

"Although no one knows who Miss Kathleen Tristan is, there are suspicions that she is Tristan's daughter from an affair he had with a peasant girl."

"I thought he didn't have any children, and having an affair isn't a common trait that martyrs share."

The driver shook his head. "We didn't know that he had a child either."

Skye got the feeling that the driver was purposely ignoring her last comment about Sir Tristan's sainthood. She quickly promised to keep her opinions to herself. After all, the residents of Virginia were very proud of Sir Tristan and his humanitarian work.

"So, why is the estate closed?" Skye was tired from the flight and wanted nothing more than for everything to make sense. She was confused, frustrated and felt as if her head may explode at any given moment.

"If there is a living descendant of Sir Tristan, the estate belongs to that individual."

Skye leaned her head against the window and closed her eyes. She thought about what the taxi driver had just said in regards to the estate's closure and wondered why she hadn't been informed about this earlier. What if she, like the public, was locked out of the estate? Where would she stay?

She opened one eye and saw the taxi's clock state 9:12 in a bright green color. Closing her tired eyes, she gave into the temptation of sleep.

Skye woke suddenly as the taxi began to shake. She looked anxiously out the window to see that they had turned off the highway and were now traveling down a dirt road. Skye felt herself being thrown around in her seat as the taxi bumped over the small stones that lay on the ground. She winced as the coarse seatbelt sliced into her stomach.

"I thought this was a tourist attraction. Don't tell me the government didn't have enough money to pay for a paved road," she muttered, more to herself than the taxi driver. Nevertheless, she received a reply.

"The government wanted to keep the estate authentic."

"Yet they were willing to add a gift shop," Skye commented.

"I'm not a politician," the driver said, obviously tired of Skye's questions and complaints. "Therefore, I have no say in what happens at the estate."

Respecting the driver's wishes to a certain degree, Skye remained quiet while entertaining the thought of *not* giving him a tip. In fact, she considered running out of the taxi and not paying him at all. No, that would never work. For one reason, he knew where she was staying.

Skye looked out the window. Darkness had fallen and the abundant rows of trees that lined the poorly maintained road were almost invisible. The road seemed to continue forever. Fear began to creep into her emotions, adding to the anxiety she already felt about driving down a deserted road with a complete stranger.

I wonder where the nearest house is. Probably miles away.

As Skye continued to watch, the large estate suddenly loomed in front of them. Everything came alive in an instant; the moon seemingly appeared out of nowhere to cast down its bright beams, while lights flickered in several rooms of the estate. The finer details were hard to see despite the lights from the moon and lanterns. This didn't upset Skye since her attention was drawn to a more interesting object – the man standing outside the imposing metal gates.

The driver rolled down his window. "Hello, I have a woman here who claims she has some sort of business to take care of in regards to the estate."

Skye felt her cheeks redden at his words. Not only was the taxi driver making her sound foolish and incompetent, he was actually putting her in danger. *The man at the gate could be anyone*, she thought angrily. *He could be a murderer or a pervert. Was it really necessary for a singular and feminine pronoun to both be used?*

"Skye Huntington?" the man at the gate leaned closer.

The taxi driver turned around in his seat and looked expectantly at Skye. It suddenly occurred to her that they hadn't introduced themselves to each other.

"Yes," she said, her voice strong and confident, just in case the man was a homicidal pervert.

"I'm Tom Dove," he replied. "I've been expecting you. I'm your historical interpreter on behalf of the Sir Tristan Estate."

"Then all plans are go?" Skye asked casually, peering at Tom through the opened window. She remembered being told that the interpreter's name was Tom Dove. She'd never speculated that he would be so handsome.

The light, which came from the lantern he held in his hands, highlighted his features. He stood tall at five foot eleven and had a lean, muscular build. His face carried his most magnificent features: blue eyes that sparkled with life and lips that formed a smile with every word he spoke. Tom's short brownish blond hair complimented his face in the most beautiful way.

"Of course the plans are still active," Tom said, breaking Skye's reverie.

Not knowing what to say next, Skye simply smiled and exited the taxi. The driver was about to step out of the vehicle as well, but Tom stopped him.

Tom took control, in an efficient yet courtly manner. "Are the lady's belongings in the trunk?"

"Yes," Skye answered.

"I'll get them," Tom offered with a smile.

Skye smiled back in appreciation and then paid the taxi driver.

"Thank you," Skye said, bidding goodbye to her short-term companion.

Skye shivered as the taxi disappeared down the dark road. *I hope there are other people in the estate.* She glanced sideways at Tom. He looked like a kind, handsome man but she didn't want to be deserted in the middle of nowhere with him.

"Let's get you inside," Tom said, stealing Skye's attention away from the empty road. "Virginian nights can get very cool."

Skye followed Tom as he placed the lantern on the ground and unlocked the gate with a large silver key. Skye bent down to pick up the lantern, and Tom had the same idea. They both knelt at the same time and almost knocked each other's head.

Tom laughed. "Would you like to carry the lantern?"

"Since you're carrying my suitcase, it's the least I can do," Skye replied.

"Sounds fair to me." Tom smiled as he locked the gate behind them.

"Am I correct in saying that you work at the Sir Tristan Estate?" Skye inquired.

"Yes. But I've only worked here for a few weeks. Although I'm new around here, I know a lot about the Tristan family."

"Since you know so much," Skye began to pry, "can you answer one question that I've been dying to know?"

Tom stopped walking and looked curiously at her. "If I can."

"What was Sir Tristan's first name?"

Tom paused, a sly smile forming on his face. "I *can* answer that question but I'm not going to – not yet."

"Why is Sir Tristan's first name so confidential?" Skye pressed. She couldn't stand not knowing. Perhaps that's why she was such a talented photographer; her attention to detail was superb.

"It's not his actual name that matters," Tom said passionately. "It is the significance of the nature of naming that matters."

"You've completely lost me," Skye said, shaking her head in confusion.

"What does a name mean to you?"

"I guess...a name describes an individual," Skye replied, after a brief pause to think about her answer.

"An individual is a human, correct?"

"I...I guess," Skye answered, startled at the obscurity of Tom's question.

"Humans are represented by their physical and emotional needs. Sir Tristan suppressed those needs in order to help others. Therefore, he doesn't need a name; he wasn't really a human. He shouldn't even be called Sir Tristan, but alas, our society feels compelled to name everything."

"Helping others should be beneficial to both parties," Skye pointed out. "Sir Tristan died in sadness."

"And your conclusion is...?"

"Although Sir Tristan helped a lot of slaves and women, it left him void of happiness and led to his demise," Skye replied. "Therefore, his actions were done...in vain?"

Skye and Tom approached the door to the estate. It loomed ten feet tall, with fine details of roses and their jagged stems engraved into the door. When Skye held up the lantern, she saw the marvelous work more clearly.

"If only Sir Tristan knew that at the time," Tom said with a heavy sigh.

"What?" Skye asked. She had been so engrossed in the design on the door that her mind was no longer concentrating on their conversation.

"If Sir Tristan knew how to live a balanced life maybe he wouldn't be doomed to come back to Earth to find that moderation." Tom used the same large silver key to open the estate's door and waited for Skye to enter. "Are you going to stand out here all night?" he asked with a laugh.

"Do you really believe that Sir Tristan's ghost has come back to look for happiness?" Skye was a believer in ghosts. She had even thought she'd seen one while photographing the interior of Sterling Castle in Scotland.

"He's back," Tom said, his voice now more formal and chilling. "But he's not only looking for happiness; he's looking for that balance I mentioned earlier."

"How do you know all of this?"

"I know all about the estate," Tom replied. He sounded like an automatic telephone recording, not the passionate individual he'd been just moments ago.

"Okay," Skye said, rubbing her hand against her forehead. "I'm really tired and I'm starting to develop a headache. Can you take me to the estate's bed and breakfast?"

"Of course," Tom said as he led her throughout a dimly lit hallway.

They reached a more modern part of the estate a few minutes later. Everything looked like a normal bed and breakfast and Skye felt her previously tense body relax as she traded the lantern for her suitcase.

"Mrs. Bradford will give you the key to your room. You should feel honored – she's been ordered to stay in the estate especially for you!"

"Poor woman," Skye muttered. "What would have happened if my flight was delayed?"

"Nothing, the owner of the estate wouldn't let her go until you came."

"Poor woman," she repeated. She stepped towards the woman behind the desk and suddenly whirled to face Tom. "Hold on a minute," she retraced her steps. "I thought the government of Virginia owned the estate."

"Not anymore. The blood relative of Sir Tristan owns the estate now. It's back in family hands, where it truly belongs."

"They found the descendant of Miss Kathleen Tristan?" Skye asked in surprise.

"Yes."

"This is too much for me to comprehend all at once," Skye said, shaking her head as if to clear her thoughts. "If you would be so kind as to explain everything tomorrow morning, I'd really appreciate it. However, I just want to sleep right now. I think I'll fall over if I don't get to a bed soon."

Tom chuckled. "All right, Ms. Huntington. Go see Mrs. Bradford; she'll show you to your room."

"Thank you for all your help!" Skye called out as Tom walked away.

"Have sweet dreams."

Tom's wishes for a good night seemed unusual to Skye. Instead of analyzing it, she decided to blame her sleep deprivation on her view of his evasive nature.

"Can I get my room please?" Skye asked.

Skye had only been asleep for an hour when she heard people shouting. The shouting was indecipherable but very nearby. Groggily, she stepped out of the bed and into her white fuzzy slippers. Just like the change in the bedroom's temperature, her slippers were suddenly very cold.

Skye tiptoed towards the bedroom door and listened silently. As her ear pressed against the cold door, she strained to hear the conversation that seemed to be happening beneath her.

"I'm sorry, Mother," Skye heard a young man say regretfully. "But I cannot marry Eleanor."

"She's a fine woman," the mother argued. "You'll never find a wife better suited for you. She's a fabulous homemaker and comes from the best breed in all of Virginia."

"Eleanor is lovely," the young man agreed. "But she is not what I want."

Skye felt her blood run cold. She was sure that the voice belonged to Tom. Unable to resist the urge to know more, she quietly opened the bedroom door and crept into the hallway.

"If you don't desire Eleanor, who *do* you want?" The woman's voice rang closer and clearer than ever before.

Skye carefully made her way to the banister and looked down. What she saw made her scream.

She was no longer looking at the bed and breakfast's front lobby, which should have been there. Instead, Skye saw an elegant, but decades old living-room. The walls and the furniture were dark and the large paintings that hung on the walls were illumined by a fireplace that crackled and glowed. The finer details of the living-room were obscured by a thin layer of fog that seemed to surround everything. It was like a mist lending an ethereal pall to the scene unfolding before her. The young man – a splitting image of Tom – and his mother were oblivious to Skye's scream. They continued their somber discussion.

"I don't want anyone or anything!" Tom cried. "I don't want to live a life that is just about personal achievement. I want more than the accumulation of wealth and status."

"Don't you dare belittle your father's work," the mother scolded. "He worked hard to make something of himself and to provide the very best for you and I."

"I am not insulting father's work," Tom interjected. "But his work enslaved many African-Americans and kept women oppressed."

"Tom thinks he's better than his parents!" the woman exclaimed. "We send you to university and this is how you repay us? You say that you want more than personal achievement and more than just money and status. Every sentence you say has the word "want" in it. You sound greedier than all the kings and queens of the world."

"You don't understand, Mother," Tom replied with the same passionate tone that Skye had heard last night. "To achieve everything I want, I must want nothing."

"You make no sense." The woman's shoulders dropped as she shook her head.

Skye watched as the woman hurried out of the room and as Tom's head fell unhappily down to his chest. Suddenly, he looked up and stared directly at Skye.

"You'll be the one to save me!" Tom cried in unbelievable pain and expectation.

Skye gasped and turned around quickly, her slippers flying from her feet. She hardly noticed their loss as she ran to the bedroom and locked the door. She jumped in the bed and threw the covers over her head, shaking in fear as she thought about what she had seen.

* * *

Skye woke up the next morning in a tangled mess of blankets. It took a full minute of twisting and turning until she was free.

She shivered as she thought about the weird dream she had last night. It was so real and scary. She concluded that it was induced by Tom's story about Sir Tristan's unusual belief system. Since Tom was the one to make her aware of Sir Tristan's belief, it was reasonable that her unconscious mind would choose him to play the part of Sir Tristan.

Skye hurried out of bed and opened the curtains. She moaned when she saw a thick layer of fog blocking the sun. Although the clock indicated that she'd slept for eight hours, she still felt tired.

Her feet grew cold against the hardwood floor, and she searched the bedroom for her white fuzzy slippers. After five minutes she gave up the search and hurried to get dressed for her breakfast appointment with Tom.

As Skye walked towards the staircase, she saw something out of the corner of her eye. She stared in disbelief.

"How in the world did my slippers get out here?" she whispered, knowing there was no one to answer.

"Hello, Skye," Tom said as she entered the bed and breakfast's dining-hall. "You look lovely."

Skye's blood went cold. Lovely was the word he'd used to describe Eleanor last night in her dream.

"That's a lie." She meant to sound friendly but her tone came out harsh. "I look awful. It feels like I haven't slept at all."

"But you did sleep," Tom stated.

"Yes," Skye said slowly. "But how would you know that?"

"The quality of our mattresses is the finest in America; everyone sleeps well here."

"If I slept so well, why do I feel so tired?"

Tom walked Skye to a nearby chair and handed her a menu. "I know just the thing to liven you up."

Skye scanned the menu. "What is it?"

"You won't find it on the menu," Tom answered. "You will, however, find it on the itinerary. How does a day of viewing some of Virginia's finest attractions sound?"

"Wonderful. Unfortunately, sight-seeing isn't
part of *my* itinerary. I should really get some work
done."

"You won't accomplish anything if you're half
asleep," Tom pointed out. "You have to let me show
you Rocky Falls. It's the most beautiful place in Virginia."

Skye glanced out the dining-hall's large window.
"I guess I would benefit from some fresh air, but it
looks like it's going to storm."

"It's not going to storm," Tom assured her. "It
won't even rain. Virginia's weather is always like
this; threatening but never producing anything
harsh."

"All right," Skye agreed, flashing her most devious smile. "I'm willing to put my assignment away
for a few hours if you show me Rocky Falls. I want
to take some pictures of Virginia for my personal
use."

"Don't you ever put your camera down?" Tom
laughed.

Tom's laugh echoed throughout the nearly empty
dining-hall. A couple of guests turned to stare at
them. Donned in professional dress, Skye guessed
that the few others staying in the bed and breakfast
were reporters.

"I love photography," Skye said, directing her attention away from the other guests and back to
Tom. "Why would I want to put my camera down?"

"Your camera can come along, but only if you allow me to buy you breakfast," Tom bargained.

"Sounds fair to me," Skye giggled like a thirteen-
year-old. She hadn't felt so excited and adventurous
in a very long time.

With a fully loaded stomach and camera, Skye followed Tom through the estate and out its metal gates.

"Are we going to walk there?" Skye asked in surprise, hurrying to keep up with Tom's fast-paced steps.

"Yes," he answered, grabbing Skye's hand and urging her to quicken her own pace.

At first Skye felt awkward with Tom holding her hand. However, as they ran through the high lush green grass, she suddenly felt completely carefree. The thick layer of fog that surrounded them caused the loss of her inhibitions. She felt as if she could do anything and not be seen.

"Are we almost there?" Skye came to an abrupt halt, making Tom stop as well. The morning dew clung to her legs as she tried to wipe it away.

"Almost, just over this hill," he replied, pulling her forward again.

"Rocky Falls is on the estate property?"

"You'll soon find out."

Skye and Tom struggled up the hill, their feet slipped and their breath came in shallow rasps.

Skye's breath caught in her throat as she reached the top of the hill and settled her eyes upon Rocky Falls.

The large waterfall loomed high in the distance. Although fog had surrounded the estate just moments ago, the air around the waterfall was clear and pure. Blue water poured down the rocky cliff face and fell at the bottom with bursts of white mist. The water ran into a small pond where it lay.

"Can we go closer?" Skye begged. The beauty of the waterfall and pond was too much for her to resist.

"Of course," Tom replied, running ahead.

Skye's legs carried her quickly over the damp, long grass until she reached Tom. She stopped at his side and took a deep breath of air so pure that she gasped in surprise.

"It's so beautiful here," Skye whispered, more to herself than Tom.

Skye leaned over the still water to see her reflection. She gasped in horror as she realized that Tom reflected no image in the pond. Skye quickly stood and turned around. She was relieved to see that Tom had moved away from the pond and was a few steps behind her. *His reflection wasn't in the pond because he wasn't there*, she thought, trying to calm her racing heart.

"What are you doing over there?" Skye asked.

"Looking at you and the waterfall. You look wonderful there. Can I take a picture of you?"

"All right," Skye handed him the camera. "You push that black button when you're ready to take the picture."

"I know how to work a camera," Tom said, rolling his eyes playfully. "All you need to worry about is looking pretty for the camera. However, I don't think that'll be too difficult for you." He winked at her, noting how she blushed and turned away to hide her face. "When you finish this role of film, you can get it developed at the estate."

"The estate has a photo lab?" Skye asked as she posed for the picture.

"Of course. The Sir Tristan Estate has everything."

"That seems to be correct," Skye observed, "especially since it's meant to be closed for business."

"Although the estate may be closed to the public, it'll always be alive."

Skye wrinkled her eyebrows. "What do you mean?"

"Smile," Tom said, ignoring her question.

Skye smiled just seconds before the camera clicked.

"Thanks," Skye said, walking forward to take the camera from Tom. "Hey!" she cried as he laughed and snapped multiple pictures of her. "Stop it!" She hated when people wasted film.

"I only took four pictures," Tom said. He looked guilty, as if he knew his behavior was inappropriate. "You can take as many roles of film as you need from the gift shop. The photo processing is free – just for you though."

Skye looked at Tom and quickly snapped a picture of him, although he didn't seem to notice. "How can you make me that offer? What's your position at the Sir Tristan Estate?"

"It's beautiful. Don't you agree?" Tom turned away from Skye and watched as the waterfall poured clear blue water.

"I agree, it's beautiful," Skye said. "But I'd like to talk about *you*."

"There's too much to tell," he replied sadly.

The fog began to envelop the waterfall and Skye shivered in the sudden coolness.

"We better get back to the estate," Skye said, noticing the vast change in Tom's disposition.

They hurried over the hill and back to the estate. This time, however, they walked in silence. Full of confusion, Skye glanced at the menacing clouds and realized she felt as bad as the weather looked.

Skye fell into bed that night with a heavy heart. Although she hadn't yet worked on her assignment, it was the least of her worries. She was more concerned about Tom, so friendly and silly one second, and then changing into a mysterious, melancholy man the next. This bipolar behavior and intensity was starting to scare her.

As Skye wrapped the thin blanket around her, she forced her mind to focus on the reason she was here. She promised herself she'd dedicate the whole of tomorrow to working on her assignment. Despite her efforts to detour her thoughts, the events of the day ominously loomed in Skye's mind as she fell into a deep sleep.

She had only been asleep for three hours when her eyes flew open. However, Skye wasn't in a dream. She felt her body being pulled forward as the voice of Tom rang throughout the hallway and into her room. This time, she had no desire to search for her white slippers even though her feet were chilled from the hardwood floor. She hurried out of the bedroom and across the hallway. As discreetly as possible, Skye peered over the banister to see Tom talking to a frightened African-American man.

The fog that surrounded Tom and the man was less dense than it had been the previous night, making it easier for Skye to view the scene in front of her. A large painting hanging on the wall caught her eye. It was of a man who looked very much like Tom, but older and sporting a thick mustache and stern expression.

"I...I can't do this," the African-American man stuttered.

Skye studied him closely. He was wearing a pair of overalls which she presumed were once white. The man looked tired and defeated; his face wore the worry that his voice projected.

"You *can* do this," Tom said forcefully.

Skye leaned further over the banister and looked closely at Tom. He looked nearly the same way he always did, but was wearing a stiff-looking suit that she had never seen before. His expression was intense and mysterious; an expression that she knew all too well.

"If Mr. Tristan finds out that you helped us escape, he'll be furious. He'll come after me and the other slaves and kill us."

"That's why you have to leave tonight. My father won't know his slaves are missing until the morning. The other slaves and you will be half way across Virginia by then. Mr. Jacobs has already loaded the others into the carriage. Your stalling is putting them all at risk."

"Will this railroad you've talked about really take us to freedom?" The man's voice was filled with so much fear and hope that Skye had to hold back her tears.

"Yes," Tom answered passionately. "You must go now or Mr. Jacobs will leave without you."

The man grabbed Tom's shoulders. "Bless you! No matter what happens to us, always be happy with your actions. You're a saint. I swear, before the end of this century you'll have changed the face of slavery forever."

"Hurry," Tom urged.

Skye watched as the soon-to-be free man hurried quietly out of the house. She stared at Tom's face; he wasn't smiling with pride over his good deed nor was he looking concerned for the slave's safety.

Now that he'd done all he could for the slaves, he looked emotionless and empty.

Through a window, Skye watched the carriage disappear into the foggy night. *There's something wrong with Tom.* She was beginning to realize that her visions weren't figments of her imagination; they told her something important about Tom's true nature. All she had to do was figure out what her dreams were trying to tell her.

* * *

Skye hurried through breakfast the next morning, anxious to start her assignment. Although Tom was supposed to be showing her around the estate, they hadn't made any definite plans. As soon as they had gotten back from Rocky Falls yesterday, Tom said goodbye and scurried off. He left Skye wondering whether his goodbye was a formal bid goodnight or a casual way of saying, "I'm leaving".

Skye walked the empty halls of the estate. *He can't leave. Whatever his job at the estate is, it seems important.*

From the map of the estate, Skye realized she was in the entertaining room. According to her map, the entertaining room was right next to the dining hall and was used to house guests before dinner was served. It was furnished with old-fashioned chairs and backless sofas. There was even a dusty brown piano in the corner. The walls were covered in nature paintings.

"They're beautiful," Skye said, her voice echoing throughout the room. This natural phenomenon suddenly made her realize how alone in the estate she really was. The only people she had seen were a few employees, all of whom had looked extremely bored.

She snapped a few pictures before entering the dining-hall. As with all the rooms in the estate, the dining-hall was decorated in an earlier period fashion and poorly lit with lanterns that hung a meter off the ground.

Skye left and moved towards the kitchen, curious to see what an old-fashioned kitchen looked like. However, she soon realized that she'd never find out as she tried, unsuccessfully, to open the locked door.

She slammed her clenched fist against the door. "The kitchen is almost as good as a dungeon when it comes to capturing hard labor." Skye continued her private tour, cursing Tom for his absence.

After three hours of work, which consisted of wandering the estate and snapping many pictures with her camera, Skye decided she had taken enough pictures for the day. She had plenty of good pictures of dark and gloomy rooms. She was particularly enthusiastic about her shots of the small rooms where Mr. Tristan had kept his slaves. She knew those pictures were the epitome of sadness.

Happy with what she had accomplished, Skye entered the estate's gift shop and headed towards the checkout.

"Hello," a clerk greeted Skye before she had even reached the checkout.

"Hi," Skye replied with a friendly smile. "Do you process film here?"

The woman nodded vigorously. "Are you Skye Huntington?"

"I was the last time I checked," Skye joked.

"Then our photographic services are free for you, Ms. Huntington," the clerk replied. "By orders of Tom Dove, of course."

"Thanks," Skye said, handing her roll of film to the clerk.

"Your pictures will be ready in one hour. Is there anything else I can get you?"

"Yes," Skye hesitated, "what is Tom's connection to the estate? I know he's a tourist guide..."

The clerk dropped the roll of film. "A tourist guide? Mr. Dove is *not* a tourist guide. He's the first owner of this estate since Sir Tristan."

Skye's eyes grew wide in response to this revelation. "Excuse me?"

"Mr. Dove is the owner of the Sir Tristan Estate," the woman repeated as she picked up Skye's roll of film.

"How...how is that possible?"

"Mr. Dove arrived at the estate a few days after the birth certificate of Kathleen Tristan was found. He had blood tests that proved him to be related to Kathleen. Therefore, the property belongs to Tom."

"This is unreal," Skye muttered, more to herself than the woman. "Why didn't he tell me that he owns the estate?"

"I don't know," the employee answered truthfully. "The knowledge of Mr. Dove's ownership was a shock to us all. He's only keeping the estate open because arrangements for reporters to visit had been made before Kathleen's birth certificate was found. All the employees are worried about losing our jobs; many have already been temporarily laid off."

Skye nodded numbly. "It must be hard for you."

"I better get started on processing your film."

"Okay," Skye said. "I'll be back in an hour."

Skye wandered out of the gift shop and towards her bedroom. She couldn't believe that Tom had kept his real identity a secret from her. With so many questions circulating in her mind, the hour passed in what seemed like a minute.

As Skye returned to the gift shop a shiver ran up and down her spine; for some unknown reason she felt as if she was being watched.

Skye observed that the estate was much quieter than it had been yesterday. She presumed that the reporters had finished their assignments and left.

"Hello again," the clerk greeted as Skye entered the gift shop for the second time that day. "Your pictures are ready."

"I could use a few more rolls of film," Skye said, taking the package. Although she had many rolls of film, she decided to take advantage of Tom's generosity

"Take as many as you like," the clerk offered.

Skye picked up three rolls of film and placed them on the counter. *She must think I'm someone important.*

The woman began to place the rolls of film in a bag as Skye hurried to place two more rolls on the counter. Her face reddened but she knew five rolls of free film were worth the embarrassment.

"Have a wonderful day," the clerk said as Skye left the gift shop.

"You too," Skye replied. However, she knew her socially appropriate comment was a waste of breath. *Who could have a wonderful day standing in an empty gift shop?*

Once in her room, Skye closed the door behind her and jumped onto the bed. She opened the package of pictures and studied them carefully. She rolled her eyes upon seeing the candid pictures of herself that Tom had taken. Skye let out a groan as she saw a picture that depicted a faraway scene of Rocky Falls. The picture looked as if it had been taken in a hurry. She tossed that picture on the ground, presuming Tom had taken it. As she flipped to the next picture, Skye realized that she was the mystery photographer, not Tom. The photograph that followed was of the estate; a picture she had taken just a few hours ago. She clearly remembered taking a picture of Tom. With shaking hands, she searched through the remaining pictures, looking for the photograph she had taken of Tom, yet she found no such picture. Skye picked up the photograph of the scenery and studied it carefully. She was positive that Tom had been standing in that exact location when she had taken the picture. Skye was a trained photographer who paid attention to even the smallest of detail, there was no way that she was mistaken. Tom *had* been standing there.

"What's going on?" As she continued to stare at the picture intensely she shook. "I have to get out of here. There's no way I'm spending another night in this estate."

Images of her strange dreams featuring Tom filled her mind. They had been so realistic that Skye began to believe they were more than just dreams. "They're waking nightmares," she realized in a shaky voice.

Her hand reached for the telephone. She was going to request a taxi come immediately. Before Skye had the chance to dial the telephone number, her body suddenly froze in terror upon hearing an ethereal voice.

"Don't leave," Tom begged from behind Skye.

With Tom's hand on top of hers, Skye shakily placed the telephone on its receiver.

"How…how did you get in my bedroom?"

Tom gave a gentle laugh. "That wasn't much of a problem."

He's acting as if this situation is normal! "How did you get in my bedroom?" Skye repeated, her voice steadier, her tone firmer.

"I used the door. What a concept, huh?" Tom took his hand off Skye and sauntered to the bed. He sat at the edge of the bed and smiled.

Skye cast a glance at the bedroom door and then did a double take. The door was locked; her slippers lay untouched in front of the door. It was impossible for him to have entered that way.

Sensing Skye's bewilderment, Tom let out a gleeful laugh and then fell backwards on the bed.

Skye knees went weak and her breath stopped when she saw Tom literally disappear into the bed. With slow, shaky steps, she looked under the bed. Tom lay under the bed, a smile on his face, his eyes locked on hers.

"Surprised?" he asked with raised eyebrows.

Skye stumbled backwards and then fell to the floor.

Tom crawled out from underneath the bed and offered his hand to Skye. She stared at his hand but didn't make any attempt to touch it.

"That wasn't an illusion…was it?"

Tom shook his head. He suddenly looked sad.

"What's going on?" Skye demanded. "If you don't tell me the truth, I'll scream so loud that Mrs. Bradford will come to my aid in a second."

"That's an exaggeration," Tom said with a weak smile as he sat down beside Skye. He noted how her body tensed in response. "Besides, your screams wouldn't yield any results. I've fired all the staff. The last employee, the woman from the gift shop, left the estate just minutes ago. We're alone."

Skye's terrified eyes darted around the room. She bit her lip.

"Don't be afraid," Tom gently urged. "I'm not going to hurt you."

"Tell me what's going on," Skye begged.

"All right," Tom sighed. "Do you remember how I told you that Sir Tristan's ghost roams the estate in search for a balanced life?"

"Yes," Skye nodded her head in harsh, jerky movements.

"Then you'll remember asking how I knew this information."

She nodded even more fiercely.

"I know because I am Sir Tristan. I'm his ghost and I've come back to life for you, Skye."

"No," Skye muttered. "No, that can't be true."

"You've just seen me float through a thick mattress and frame, yet you don't believe me? I thought you were a believer in ghosts."

"I do believe but I just don't understand any of this. I thought your name was Tom Dove."

"My name is Tom Dove," Tom replied sadly. "Tom Dove Tristan. Surely you remember asking what Tristan's first name was. Now you know."

"The woman at the gift shop said you were a descendant of Kathleen Tristan's. Are you really her father?"

"Yes," Tom answered, blushing furiously and dropping his head to his chest in shame. "Everything I told you about my previous life was true. I was a martyr. All I cared about was living a life that served others. However, I went too far and dedicated all of my time to the cause. In the process, I led a miserable personal life and hurt my family. I didn't know what was wrong with me; I had these uncontrollable urges to help others. I didn't find out until my third life that I have a personality disorder. By some divine intervention, I've been sent back to

Earth to try and lead a balanced life. At first, I was sent back to the time in which I lived. However, I went overboard in my quest for happiness. I was so ready to live a life full of excitement that I got a peasant girl pregnant." Tom rubbed his right hand against his forehead. He was sweating and was obviously uncomfortable in revealing this information.

Skye felt her stomach churn. She was disgusted at Tom's actions. "That's why the birth certificate of Kathleen Tristan has shown up just recently in the estate. It did just happen recently." She creased her forehead in concentration; her reasoning made sense to her.

"You're right," Tom agreed. "When I was unable to live a balanced life in the eighteen hundreds, I was sent to the present. I proved myself to be related to Kathleen Tristan and regained my estate. Now, I'm going to live a balanced life. I won't disappoint the power that has given me so many chances. Will you help me finally live my life, Skye?"

Skye's mouth opened, but no reply was uttered. She looked at the bed and back at Tom. "You want me to marry a ghost?"

"Yes," Tom pleaded. "Please say you'll marry me. Think of all the fun we had at Rocky Falls. Imagine having an eternity to do nothing but roam the grounds of my estate."

"Those dreams," she muttered, looking at Tom for an explanation.

"I did that," Tom confessed. "Those were memories of my first life. You said you wanted to know all about Sir Tristan and his estate. I was giving you the best tour anyone could ever hope to experience."

Skye slowly lifted herself off the cold hardwood floor. Tom smiled and reached out his hand. This time, Skye took it. She waited until he was almost standing up when she pushed him backwards. Tom let out a startled cry and fell to the ground.

"Get away from me!" Skye cried. "I'll never marry you." She flung the bedroom door open and ran as fast as she could. Her legs darted so fast down the stairs that she almost fell. However, she managed to keep her balance as she landed at the bottom of the stairs.

"Come back!" Tom yelled. "You're going to be the one to save me!"

No, I'm not, Skye thought while racing through the empty lobby as fast as she could. Reaching the large carved entrance door, she used all her weight to pull it open. Her blood went cold. There, blocking her way to freedom and safety, was Tom.

"Don't try to run, Skye." Although Tom was begging, there was a hint of threat in his voice.

"Let me go!" Skye cried. Tears formed in her eyes as Tom grabbed her by the waist.

"I can't do that," Tom replied simply. "You're going to be the one to keep me balanced."

"Medication can do that!" Skye yelled as she kicked Tom in his groin.

Instinctively, Tom released her and groaned in pain. "That hurt."

Skye felt herself being drawn to Tom's eyes. When she gave heed to the feeling, she gasped in horror. His eyes had become completely black. She turned around as fast as she could and then ran back into the building. Knowing it would be a useless attempt, she didn't bother locking the door – Tom could walk right through it.

"Come back here," Tom growled in a tone Skye had never heard before.

Ignoring Tom's command, she continued to run. Skye sped past the many storage rooms. She had been down in this part of the estate earlier today while taking photographs and remembered there was another exit just past the small rooms where the slaves used to live. All she had to do was reach the exit and run down the road to freedom.

Skye had just entered the dimly lit hallway, where the slave rooms began, when she heard Tom call to her.

"Don't try to escape, Skye, you're going to stay with me forever. I promise I'll treat you well. You'll have everything that you've always wanted."

Except freedom, Skye thought as she slid through a door that was slightly ajar. The slave room was darker than the hallway and the only light came through a missing brick in the wall.

Skye scanned the room, searching for a place to hide but the room was empty. She considered finding somewhere else to hide when a voice from behind startled her.

"I helped the slaves escape."

"I know," Skye said. Her breathing was labored, her hair clumped and matted with sweat.

"Aren't you proud of me?" Tom's expressions changed rapidly from anger to sadness to happiness.

Skye stood taller, no longer as afraid. She brushed a clump of matted hair from her face. *He doesn't just suffer from a personality disorder, he's seriously ill.*

Tom extended a shaking hand. "It's time to go to our wedding," he pleaded. "Let's get married right now!"

From the moment she met him, Skye was aware of Tom's peculiar and erratic behavior. However, that was just a taste of what she was experiencing now. Skye was terrified at his sudden change in personality.

"Okay," she replied, unable to disguise the tremor in her voice. "Let's get married." Skye knew she had no chance to escape while cornered in the slave's room. She planned to go along with whatever Tom said until she could run away.

Tom smiled and took Skye's hand. Her blood ran cold at his touch.

His free hand took the moist tresses of her hair and sensuously rubbed them on his cheek. "We're going to be so happy."

"Can we have the wedding outside?" Skye suggested, forcing a smile.

Tom smiled and squeezed her hand so hard she feared it would break. "Whatever you want, Skye. This is wonderful! I'll marry us; we don't need a minister."

"Yes, you can marry us," she urged Tom forward.

"All right!" Tom cried happily, hugging her tightly.

As Skye and her ghostly fiancée walked out of the basement, her mind raced for options.

"I have to get a dress. Does your mother have one I could borrow?"

"Oh yes, she has many dresses. They are all in my room. I'll take you to them."

Tom urged Skye up the stairs. She had to take two stairs at a time as Tom excitedly hurried her along.

"In here," Tom said, opening the door to his bedroom. "The dresses are in that brown closet over there." He pointed to a large closet and then smiled at Skye. "You'll make a beautiful bride."

"Thank you," Skye said, closing the door. She hurried to the closet and was about to open it when something on a nearby counter caught her eye. Upon closer examination, she realized that it was a weekly pillbox. Carefully opening the lids, she discovered that Tom had missed several days of his medication.

Skye felt like a ton of bricks had just hit her. She'd been so confused at the change in Tom's personality but now she realized that the change was due to not taking his medication. Clearly, Tom was inflicted with a severe personality disorder, but could act perfectly normal – as long as he took his medication. Skye could hardly believe the thoughts she was having. *A ghost that needs medication?* Although she now knew the reason for the problem, the realization wasn't much help for her current situation. Skye knew she needed to get out of the house immediately and that she was wasting precious time.

"Are you almost ready, dear?" Tom asked.

At the sound of Tom's voice, Skye jumped and dropped the case of pills. "Almost!" she called.

"Hurry, my dear. The guests have started to arrive."

Skye's heart raced faster. *His condition is rapidly getting worse.* She looked outside the bedroom window to see an empty garden surrounded by fog. *He thinks there are guests outside! Then again, he is a ghost. Maybe there are ghost guests out there.* That thought made her shiver, the chill consuming her entire body.

Terrified, Skye stood in the middle of the room as tears began to roll down her face. Her situation seemed hopeless; her body shook with sobs of despair. Just as she felt as if she was going to collapse, a loud beep from a car horn echoed in her ears.

Huh? Skye looked out the window. A wide smile spread across her face as she saw the taxi driver, the same one who had brought her to this terrible estate, exit the car and head towards the door.

Skye flung open the window and yelled for help. "I'm up here! Please, you have to help me!"

"Be quiet!" Tom roared from behind the door.

The taxi driver heard the scared and angry shouts and looked up to see Skye waving furiously from the window.

"Help me!" Skye yelled, even louder this time.

Tom kicked the door open and stormed into the room. Skye spun around in fear and saw Tom's eyes blazing with anger.

She ran through the open door, startling Tom in the process. She heard Tom's feet pound against the stairs as he followed her.

Skye was almost out of breath when she reached the exit and pulled open the door. Tom was so close behind her that she could feel his cold breath on her neck.

The taxi driver was waiting anxiously outside as Skye burst through the door.

"Are you all right?" the driver asked as she grabbed onto him.

"He's the ghost of Sir Tristan!" Skye cried, pointing at Tom. "That *is* Sir Tristan."

"That...that can't be," the driver stuttered.

"It is," Skye shrieked as Tom moved forward, an angry expression on his face.

"Don't move another inch!" the driver commanded.

Tom ignored him and continued forward.

"What do you want?" the driver asked with less confidence. He and Skye stepped backwards as Tom advanced.

"I want my bride," Tom demanded.

The driver cast Skye a confused glance.

"It's not true. He's a mentally ill ghost who forgot to take his medication."

The driver's eyes went wide as Tom reached forward and purposely floated his hand through his throat.

"You're a ghost!" The driver ran to the taxi and jumped inside. Skye was close at his heels. He fumbled with the key, his hands shaking so badly he couldn't insert it.

"Hurry," Skye begged. She looked up to see Tom's arms float through the front window. His hands were reaching straight for her.

"Stay with me forever," Tom begged. "Please put an end to my suffering."

Skye screamed as Tom's cold hands grasped her shoulders.

Tom's hands suddenly flew away. The driver had finally started the engine and put the car into reverse. The car sped backwards, leaving Tom standing in the road, shaking his fists as the dust swirled around him.

"Come back!" Tom pleaded as he chased the moving car.

"He's going to catch us – go faster," Skye begged.

The taxi driver floored the pedal and they watched as Tom disappeared in the distance.

"That...that was unreal!" the driver stuttered as the car left the unpaved road and merged into traffic.

"I know," Skye agreed with a shiver. "When I found out who Tom Dove really was, I said the exact same thing."

"Will he follow us?" The driver glanced at Skye, his face filled with worry.

"I don't think so. Somehow I don't think he could bear to leave his estate."

"What happened in there?"

"It's all too much to explain," Skye began. "But what I will say is that you saved my life. If you hadn't shown up..." she let her voice trail off. She didn't want to think about still being trapped in the estate with Tom Dove Tristan. "Why *did* you come?" Skye asked curiously.

"To give you this," the driver said, stopping at a red light and passing her a roll of film.

"Where did you get this?"

"You must have dropped it while you were in my taxi. Since you mentioned that you're a professional photographer, I thought it might be important."

Skye held the roll of film in her hand. "It's the most important roll of film I've ever had because it saved my life!" *I guess photography really is my true calling. At least it had better be. I'm so out of a job once I return home with a half finished assignment.*

"Don't worry about losing your job," the driver reassured Skye, as if reading her thoughts. "You'll come and live with me. You can take pictures of the beautiful scenery that Virginia has to offer."

Skye felt the familiar feeling of her blood going cold. "How...how did you know what I was thinking?"

"I'm a sorcerer. I only drive a taxi to pay my rent. Sorcery is my first love. However, most women find me weird – it gets really lonely. Since you've already seen the unnatural, maybe you won't find me so scary. What do you say, Skye?"

Skye's hand reached for the door handle as she prepared to jump out of the moving car. It snapped shut. She looked at the driver with wide eyes.

"I can read minds, remember?" the driver said with a smile. "We're going to have so much fun."

Skye furiously jerked on the door handle, cursing when it wouldn't budge. *I wish I'd never accepted the assignment.*

"Getting away from me won't be easy," the driver scolded. "I can foresee everything and right now I'm seeing you and me together for a very long time!"

I should have stayed with Tom, she thought glumly.

"I heard that."

* * *

Freaky Frank

Twenty-year-old Brittany Addams looked around the carnival grounds in confusion. Although she held a map of the carnival in her hands, she was still completely lost. As Brittany stood there, unsure of what to do next, her thoughts traveled to the event that had led her to the carnival in the first place.

It had all started on the day that Brittany learned she wouldn't have a job for the summer. For the last four summers she'd worked at Kid Kare. Kid Kare was a university sponsored day care program that looked after elementary school kids while their parents worked. It was also what Brittany relied on for employment. When she learned that Kid Kare was shutting down due to the change of direction in the university's plan, Brittany was shocked. And because she heard the disappointing news so late in the spring, she had very little time to search for a good paying job. The result was the eventual acceptance of a job at the local summer carnival.

"You seem lost. Can I help you?"

Brittany turned around quickly, startled that someone was behind her. She had to suppress a gasp when her eyes settled upon the man who had spoken. In her opinion, he was the most handsome man she'd ever seen. The stranger stood tall at five foot eleven. He had, what Brittany imagined, a well-built body underneath his loose fitting blue and black plaid shirt and dark blue jeans. The man had dark curly hair which was cut relatively short. A well-kept mustache made his face all the more mysterious and exciting. Although every aspect of the man seemed above average, it was his eyes that marveled Brittany. They were a brilliant color of blue; a shade so intense they screamed that this man had a secret — one that teased Brittany and enticed her to get closer.

"Can I help you with anything?" An amused smile played upon the man's lips.

"I...I'm looking for the training pavilion."

"A newbie, huh?"

"Yeah. I was meant to be at the pavilion five minutes ago, but I can't find it. It's my first day as well. I can't imagine how bad my tardiness must seem." Brittany felt her face growing red as she talked. It was funny how tongue-tied she could be one moment, and then go on rambling the next. *It's probably a defective gene*, she thought to herself, fully aware of her change in speech.

The man smiled again, showing that he understood her uneasiness. "Don't worry so much. After all, this *is* a carnival."

"I hope you're right."

"Nevertheless, I'm sure Mr. Watson would want you to show up sometime today."

"Oh, I'll show up. It just might take me a few hours to find the damn place!"

The man laughed and then offered Brittany his hand. "I'm Frank Stanford."

She reached out and shook his hand. "My name is Brittany."

"I'm very pleased to meet you, Brittany. I'd love to chat longer but I'd better get you to the training pavilion now."

Brittany nodded although she felt a hint of disappointment. "That's probably a good idea."

Brittany and Frank didn't say much as they hurried through the carnival grounds. In the silence, Brittany wondered why her emotions were suddenly having an internal war. She was almost mad at herself for developing such an intense attraction to Frank. *Don't get your hopes up,* she thought to herself. It was typical of her to focus all her attention on a particular guy. Each time concluded with the same result: heartache.

"Here's the place you were looking for," Frank said suddenly, stopping at a large white tent. "Do you want me to explain why you're late? I know Mr. Watson very well so it won't be any trouble at all."

"It's all right." Brittany was really touched by Frank's concern and the effort he'd offered to extend to her.

"Your prerogative," Frank said casually as he turned to leave. He paused for a moment and then turned around. "Don't be a stranger, Brittany."

Brittany felt her heart rate increase as she watched Frank walk away. *He's hot!* It was at that moment in time she decided she wanted to see more of Frank.

* * *

Brittany didn't see Frank for the remainder of the week. She was stuck in a little office where she learned the finer points of operating the educational movie theater. Whenever Mr. Watson referred to the dark tent, twenty-inch screen and twelve person seating arrangement as a "movie theater", Brittany had to suppress a laugh. She knew the carnival only hosted the PTA's idea for an educational movie theater to please the municipal government. Perhaps that was why Mr. Watson was so lackadaisical in Brittany's training. He'd even confessed to her that the same movie, produced in the early 1990's, was played every year. When Brittany asked him why the movie wasn't viewed by anyone, Mr. Watson replied by asking her if she'd want to see a movie on the formation of fungus. He'd never waited to hear her answer for he already knew what it would be.

During her time apart from Frank, Brittany had begun to realize that her feelings for him were entirely superficial. She almost felt embarrassed by the way he consumed her mind. Brittany knew she was acting like she had a preteen crush; clearly not her strongest quality. Although she still wanted to get to know Frank and perhaps engage in some harmless flirting, she knew she had to be sensible about it. Her feelings had to stay right where they were – on the surface. Nevertheless, the fact that she had to keep telling herself to keep her emotions at bay undoubtedly indicated that she just might fall for him.

As Brittany left the carnival grounds on Friday night, she sighed heavily, although she wasn't sure why. Part of her was happy that her training was over and that she would be able to interact with the public next week. However, the other part of Brittany was worried about bumping into Frank. Against her foremost will, he'd already won a place in her heart. If he'd already affected her so deeply within the few minutes they had spent together, what would an hour, a day, a week, do to her? Even worse, what if he broke her heart like so many men had done before?

* * *

Brittany spent the weekend with her best friend, Amanda Finley. They window-shopped their way through the better part of Saturday at the mall and then relaxed by Amanda's pool on Sunday.

Brittany had always envied Amanda. In her eyes, Amanda had everything. Mr. Finley was a successful lawyer while Mrs. Finley was a stay-at-home mom who was heavily involved in the PTA. Although Amanda's home and life were filled with expensive items and trips, they truly were molded from the traditional 1950's family stereotype. Brittany knew that the Finleys would stick together through thick or thin.

Lucky for them, Brittany thought, *they have only experienced the thickness of life.*

In comparison to the Finleys, the Addams seemed like a family from the 1930's. There was always a great depression in Brittany's house, which was caused by one of several fights. Mr. Addams' contract jobs left him out of work every year or so and Mrs. Addams was underpaid as a waitress. Although there was familial love underneath the Addams problems, it never raised to the surface as much as Brittany would like it to.

"You seem distracted," Amanda noted as she sipped her chilled Alaskan water. "Is there something on your mind?"

"Not really," Brittany lied.

Amanda raised a thin eyebrow at Brittany but said nothing.

Brittany looked at Amanda, secretly hoping she'd push her to confess what was really on her mind.

When Amanda failed to hound her, Brittany spoke up voluntarily.

"I've met someone at work." The words felt weird as they left Brittany's mouth. They seemed odd because they hinted at something that wasn't completely true. She hardly knew Frank, after all.

"That was fast! Who is he?"

"Well, I hardly know him."

"Does he even know who you are?" Amanda didn't give Brittany a chance to respond. "You always do this, Brit. You fall for some guy who hardly knows you exist. You *really* have to stop blowing things out of proportion."

Brittany felt her face burn in anger. Although she'd always suspected that Amanda thought her to be fickle, Brittany wasn't prepared to hear the hurtful words come from her mouth.

"Don't look so hurt," Amanda demanded lightly. "I know this sounds awful, but I have to be cruel to be kind. It's best that you know the truth. And the truth is that you fall too hard, too quickly."

Brittany looked at Amanda and felt her anger disappear. Although Amanda could've phrased her concern in a nicer way, she *was* trying to help.

"You're right," Brittany said finally, trying desperately to keep her dignity intact. "I wear my heart on my sleeve."

"Just keep it tucked under your jacket where it will be harder for thieves to steal it." Amanda stood up, smiled at her friend and then dove into the pool.

Brittany closed her eyes, thinking about Amanda's words. They echoed in her mind and remained there until she fell asleep that night.

* * *

It was a beautiful, sunny Monday morning. The sky was bright blue and there wasn't a cloud in sight. Brittany was enjoying her first day as a trained employee. The job, which consisted of sitting outside a white tent and taking the non-existent customers' tickets, was extremely favorable in Brittany's eyes.

The educational film tent was located deep within the carnival grounds, in a space surrounded by an information booth and a first aid center. Due to the obscure location, fun-seeking carnival goers were seldom there. Although the job was easy, Brittany was beginning to get bored. She made a mental note to bring a novel to work tomorrow.

Brittany's heart began to race in an unexpected excitement as she saw Frank walking towards the educational film tent. Her eyes feasted on him as he walked towards her with a half-friendly, half-mysterious smile on his face. He wore a green and white plaid shirt and dark blue jeans. Brittany suddenly found herself appreciating plaid like she had never done before.

"Hi."

"Hey, Brittany. I told you not to be a stranger. Where have you been all week?"

"I've been busy with Mr. Watson." Brittany couldn't help but stare into Frank's eyes. They were just so beautiful. She snapped back to reality upon hearing Frank laugh.

"Your comment about being busy with Mr. Watson sounded like an innuendo." Frank brought his laughter to a calm chuckle. "Don't go around telling people that. They won't take it as innocently as I."

"Of course I meant it in an innocent manner." Brittany was blushing fiercely.

"I'm glad. That kind of behavior wouldn't be tolerated on these grounds."

"What do you mean?"

"I mean that a romance between an employer and an employee would be very scandalous. A 9.5 on the carnival Richter scale."

"How about an employee-employee romance?" Brittany asked before she even had time to think about what she was saying.

"That's tolerable," Frank said with mischievous eyes that burned into Brittany's.

Brittany coughed unnecessarily. She began to wonder if she was being too blunt with Frank. "Uh, so what do you do at the carnival anyway?"

"I operate my own attraction," Frank said with pride. "I run a freak show."

Brittany felt her breath catch in her throat. She didn't know how she felt about Frank's attraction. Brittany hated to think that his job made anyone feel badly about themselves.

"Relax," Frank said casually, noticing the bewildered expression on her face. "My freak show is run in good faith. No animals are hurt and no humans are ever part of the show – expect for me, of course."

Brittany forced herself to smile with Frank.

"Stanford's Freaky Shriek's Freak Show has been in the family for years. It's a wonderful business when you know what you're doing."

"Know what you're doing?"

"Yeah. You need to know where to find unusual creatures."

"Your creatures are real? I thought freak shows were just fake – an excuse for someone to sew a duplicate head onto a sheep's wool." Brittany giggled to herself, unable to suppress the unusual image she'd created in her head.

Frank's intense eyes locked on Brittany. Although he looked a little bit upset, he didn't look mad.

"All the creatures in my show are real. I'm a man of my word and would never willingly cheat someone."

"What type of creatures do you have?" Brittany was still unsure if Frank was joking or not.

"I could tell you but I'd rather show you."

"It just so happens that I have a lunch break starting right now." Brittany cast Frank what she hoped was a flirty, playful smile.

"I'd rather show you my exhibit after work. There are so many things that I don't think we'd get through it all in half an hour."

"After work sounds fine. So, what do you do for work in the winter?" Brittany asked as she and Frank headed towards the staff's lunch tent.

"I travel part of the time."

"And for the rest of the winter?"

"My exhibit has a winter home in the city. It could be a permanent arrangement, but I prefer it not to be."

"Why?"

"I like to be outdoors." Frank ushered Brittany into the lunch tent. "I like to discover new places and creatures."

"I still don't understand how you find creatures for your freak show," Brittany stated as she grabbed her homemade lunch from the refrigerator. She felt a strange connection to Frank when she saw him do the same.

"You'll understand once you've seen my show. Everything will be a lot clearer then."

"I'll just have to take your word for it."

"That's one thing you can always count on."

Painfully, Brittany pulled her eyes away from Frank's. The tent was busy and she didn't want people to see Frank and herself gazing lovingly into each other's eyes.

"There aren't any tables left," Brittany pointed out.

"Perhaps we could go to the educational film tent and eat there."

Brittany felt a shiver of excitement run up and down her spine as she thought about being alone with Frank. "Great idea."

A pleasant breeze swept through the tent as Brittany and Frank contently ate their homemade sandwiches. They had hardly spoken on the walk over to the tent and were just as silent now. Every few minutes or so, Brittany would steal a glance at Frank. Since she was sitting relatively close to him, she could see the faint wrinkles underneath his eyes, making her question his age. Stirred by that unanswered question, Brittany began to realize that she hardly knew the man she was sharing her lunch break with.

"How old are you?"

"I'm thirty-six. You look like you're in your early twenties, am I right?"

"Twenty."

Frank smiled proudly. "I'm good at reading these types of things about people. Age is just one of my specialties."

"Along with modesty." Brittany rolled her eyes and then laughed to show that she was only kidding.

"You have beautiful eyes."

Brittany stopped laughing; her face turned serious. "You have beautiful eyes as well. Are you married?"

"No." Frank looked a bit taken aback by Brittany's straight-forwardness.

"Why not?"

"My lifestyle, mainly. I had to work very hard to get where I am now. My traveling schedule is also a bit unpredictable."

"Although those are legit reasons, I feel like you're using them as an excuse."

"You're right. I would incorporate a woman into my hectic life if I really wanted to. The sad part is that I've never wanted a woman badly enough to make that sacrifice. I know this sounds pathetic, but I've never really been in love."

Brittany looked at Frank intensely. She was surprised to find her eyes filled with tears. She was at once both deeply touched and extremely excited. She'd never felt so close to another human being in all her life. Unable to resist the urges she felt inside herself, Brittany rose from her chair and leaned towards Frank.

Frank mimicked Brittany's actions, but with more vigor. He pressed his chest and his lips against hers. In the middle of the educational film tent, they held each other close.

"You're so beautiful," Frank muttered into Brittany's hair as he held her tightly. "I've wanted to do this ever since I laid my eyes upon you." After his declaration of appreciation, he brought his lips to Brittany's once again.

"I don't think the PTA had *that* type of education in mind," a voice said from the tent's entrance.

Brittany jumped away from Frank quickly. She felt her face go a deep shade of red as she looked at a slightly amused Mr. Watson.

"I'm so sorry," Brittany muttered in embarrassment. "I didn't plan for any of this to happen, honest."

"What exactly did happen?"

"Absolutely nothing," Frank confirmed.

"You don't have to convince me," Mr. Watson said with a smile as he left the tent.

"That was embarrassing," Frank said after a moment's pause.

"Yeah." Brittany hoped that she wasn't in any trouble with Mr. Watson. After all, kissing a man almost twice your age in the educational film tent you're meant to be operating isn't very professional. "Perhaps you should go."

"Do you want me to go?"

"Not exactly, but I think you should. My lunch break is over now anyway."

"All right," Frank said as he turned around to leave. With shoulders slumped, he slowly began to make his way to the exit.

"Frank?" Brittany called before he left the tent.

"Yes?"

"Come back after closing tonight. You promised to show me your freak show, remember?"

"Of course," Frank answered, his lips curving into a devious smile. "See you then."

Brittany shivered in excitement as she watched Frank walk away. Although she was afraid she'd be in trouble, the whole situation was pretty daring — especially for her.

As the day went on, Brittany realized that Mr. Watson hadn't exaggerated about the educational film tent's lack of popularity. Only a grandmother, along with her bored-looking grandson, had come by, and it was questionable whether they watched the film at all or just wanted to sit in the theatre for a break. Brittany wondered how the carnival could afford to pay for her presence at such an unsuccessful booth.

"Hello Brittany, how are things going?"

Brittany jumped when she heard the voice from behind her. She turned around fast to reveal Mr. Watson standing at the tent's entrance. *He has to stop popping out of nowhere,* she thought, her teeth clenched and heart racing.

"Things are going fine. I had two customers today."

"Two?" Mr. Watson asked with wide eyes as he came closer to Brittany. "You've beaten last year's record in just a day."

"Stop joking," Brittany said in an uneasy voice. Although she was referring to Mr. Watson's comment about her breaking the record, the two word sentence also spoke of her desire for him to stop coming closer.

"I'm not joking. You're naturally charismatic."

"That doesn't make sense. There's no need to say naturally before charismatic. It's a natural trait..."

"I'll have to think up another word that starts with the letter N to put in front of charismatic." By now he'd backed Brittany into a corner of the tent. Mr. Watson placed his hands above Brittany's head and leaned them against the thin canvas wall. "Naughty starts with an N. Yes, that's what you are. You're a little naughty charismatic girl."

Brittany felt her face flush red in fear and anger. "Excuse me? I'm not naughty nor a little girl."

"I know you're not a little girl – that's just a figure of speech. You're all woman to me."

"Get off me!" Brittany cried in disgust as Mr. Watson leaned in close and tried to push his body against hers.

"Come on, Brittany. I know you're the carnival's resident slut. Frank isn't any better than me, so give me what he got."

"You bastard!" Brittany lifted her leg and kneed Mr. Watson in the groin. At instant contact, Mr. Watson released his grasp and groaned, his hands flying towards his crotch and his knees buckling.

Taking the opportunity of escape which her actions had yielded, Brittany ran across the tent and out through its door. She was hardly a foot from the tent when she bumped into Frank.

"Hey! What's going on?" Frank asked in surprise as Brittany tried to hide behind him. "Are you okay?"

"No." Brittany was almost in tears. "I was alone in the tent when Mr. Watson came in and tried to force himself on me."

"Did he hurt you?"

"Not really. He certainly frightened me though."

"That's enough of a reason for me," Frank seethed as he hurried into the tent with Brittany at his heels. "What the hell is going on?"

Mr. Watson looked up from where he was sitting. He held the two used carnival tickets in his hands. "I'm getting the day's takings. What does it look like I'm doing?"

"You look like you're wallowing in rejection after trying to attack an employee."

"Frank, Frank, Frank," Mr. Watson muttered as he stood up from the chair he was sitting in. "You know as well as I do that she's nothing more than a slut. You can't blame me for trying to get what you got earlier today."

Brittany's mouth fell open in shock. Although she was completely offended by Mr. Watson's words, Frank seemed even more insulted. A look of fury washed over his face as he raised his fist and brought its wraith upon Mr. Watson. Mr. Watson stumbled back a few feet and then moaned in pain. A trickle of blood trailed down his face from his nose.

"You truly are a freak, Frank!" Mr. Watson gently rubbed his swelling face.

"I'm not the freak, you are," Frank retorted in disgust. "You're a desperate old pervert who doesn't understand the word no. You don't deserve the love of a damn dog."

Brittany could sense that Frank was getting ready to hit Mr. Watson again. Not wanting Frank to go overboard and get into serious trouble, she moved towards him and placed her hand on his arm.

"If you ever so much as look at Brittany again, you'll be in one hell of a state."

"Is that a threat?"

"It's a threat all right and one I'd be more than happy to carry out."

"Come on, buddy. We've been friends for almost a year. Don't blow it all for a foolish carnival worker."

Frank looked at Brittany for a moment, trying to calm himself down. Then he turned to Mr. Watson and forced him into the corner that Brittany had occupied just minutes ago. The tent shook so furiously at the impact that Brittany was afraid it would topple over.

"I'm not your friend and I never will be! Get out of my face. I never want to see you again."

Brittany watched as Mr. Watson shot them a dirty look and then hurried out of the tent. The silence that followed his exit seemed louder than the yelling that was present just moments ago. Brittany slowly pulled Frank close to her and then embraced him.

They stood there, holding each other, for several minutes.

"Thank you," Brittany said finally, her head buried into Frank's chest.

"He's a worthless jerk. Disregard everything he's ever said."

"I already have. How could I possibly think about anything else than what you've just done for me?"

"It was nothing."

"It means everything to me," Brittany said, looking at Frank with misty eyes. "The way you hit Mr. Watson was so hot."

Brittany and Frank laughed. He stroked her hair gently and then pulled her in for a kiss.

"Are you okay?" Frank was still holding Brittany tightly as she nodded. "Then I really think you should report what happened. Don't let him get away with what he's done."

"What if Mr. Watson reports what you did in retaliation?"

"I don't care if he reports what I've done. Don't let my actions stop you."

"Okay." Brittany let her hands fall from Frank's waist. "I'll go now."

"Want me to come with you?"

Brittany nodded shyly. "Will you walk with me to the main office?"

"Of course."

As Brittany and Frank walked across the carnival grounds together, Brittany thought about how ironic her day had been. Although she was very insulted by Mr. Watson, she was also very honored by Frank's subsequent actions.

* * *

Brittany woke up late the next morning. At first she didn't remember the events of the day before, but within a few minutes they came flooding back to her. She'd reported everything that had happened with Mr. Watson yesterday. The person who she'd talked to took down her name and telephone number and promised to investigate the matter thoroughly. Brittany hadn't received any telephone calls from the carnival supervisor and was left wondering if she was expected to work today.

The clock read 9:10 AM. Brittany was already late, but she didn't care. After all, she had no desire to impress her former trainer and boss. Unsure of what to do next, yet not wanting to be unreliable, Brittany quickly got dressed, had breakfast and hurried to the carnival grounds.

It was an unusually cool morning for the beginning of July. The sky looked threatening, as if it could rain at any second. When Brittany reached the educational film tent she was surprised to see a yellow and black sign that read "closed".

"So much for keeping me informed," Brittany muttered. "What the hell am I suppose to do now?"

"Forget it all for a while and have some fun."

Brittany jumped when she heard the voice coming from behind her. "Frank, you scared me!"

"Sorry." Frank gave Brittany a hug and a kiss on the cheek.

"They didn't even tell me that the educational film tent was closed. I should've stayed home."

"I'm glad you came. I can show you my freak show now."

"I should probably find out what's going on with my job."

"Shall I walk you to the office?"

"No!" Brittany said sharply, startling Frank in the process. "Why should I? They didn't have the decency to tell me the educational film tent was closed."

"To my freak show then?" Frank asked with raised eyebrows.

"To the freak show."

Brittany and Frank walked past the many colorful stands and rides. They were beginning to approach what she thought was the edge of the carnival's property.

"I've never been to this part of the carnival," Brittany said with a slight shiver. "I didn't even know it existed. How can you get any business with a location like this? It's harder to find than the educational film tent." Brittany knew she was rambling but she couldn't help it. This area of the carnival was very deserted. The dark clouds in the gray sky did nothing to calm her nerves.

"I get a lot of business. The money is really great."

"It is? I didn't think there was much money to be made from carnival stands."

"My exhibit is much more than a stand," Frank said mysteriously.

Brittany and Frank stopped talking, but continued to walk at a fast pace.

"Are we almost there?" Brittany finally asked.

"It's at the bottom of this hill."

Brittany stared at the steep hill that lay before them and sighed.

"Come on, you'll survive the exercise," Frank said with a laugh as he took Brittany's hand.

Brittany's hand stayed in Frank's until they were half way down the hill. When they reached the bottom, she sucked in her breath suddenly, trying to take in the sight before her.

"Oh my gosh!" Brittany's eyes went wide as they looked upon the large tent that lay at the bottom of the hill. The tent was a long rectangle, at least five hundred feet long and a hundred feet wide. The exterior was a dark shade of gray and looked much sturdier than the other tents that littered the carnival grounds.

"Frank, is this really all yours?"

"Yes," Frank said with excited eyes that seemed to glow despite the lack of sunshine. "But the exterior is nothing compared to what lies within."

Nothing more was said as Brittany and Frank continued forward. The closer they got to the tent, the larger and more mysterious it seemed.

"Come in," Frank gestured with his hands, opening the entrance to the tent.

As Brittany stepped into the tent her eyes went wide and then she began to laugh. The tent was divided into sections, making the room she was in very small. A line of lights revealed the littleness of the room. Her laughter stemmed from the display in the middle of the room.

"Take a closer look," Frank said, running to the large fish tank and smiling proudly. He didn't seem the least bit offended by Brittany's laughter.

Brittany cast Frank a confused look and then peered into the tank. It looked like an ordinary fish tank filled with clear water, blue pebbles at the bottom, live green plants, a miniature ship and, of course, fish. Brittany continued to watch the small fish swim back and forth for several minutes.

"They're pretty but what's so special about them?"

"Do you want to see what makes them so freaky?" Frank asked so passionately that he scared Brittany. "Tell the fish your name."

"Excuse me?" Brittany would've laughed if Frank hadn't looked so serious.

"Just tell them your name."

"Okay, fish," Brittany said, feeling incredibly stupid. "My name is Brittany Addams." She gasped as soon as she'd finished speaking. The lights had suddenly gone out.

Frank's voice came from the darkness. "I turned off the lights so you could see my academic fish."

"Your academic fish? What type of breed is that?" Brittany's voice trailed off as she stared at the fish. They looked as if they were glowing in the dark. They'd stopped swimming back and forth and were now gathering together in the middle of the tank. "What's...what's going on?" Brittany felt her whole body shake as she watched the glowing fish form the letter B.

Frank put his hand on Brittany's shoulder. "You'll see."

Brittany's breath came out in shallow rasps as she watched the fish form R, I, T, T, A, N, Y. The fish swam in a unified motion until they had spelled the word Brittany with their bodies. Brittany's name lingered in the tank for a while and then it was replaced with the name Addams.

Brittany was in a daze as Frank turned the lights back on. "That...that has to be some sort of trick."

"It's not. It's all natural. I don't use any form of control over these fish or any of the other creatures."

"This is *not* natural and it's definitely not normal."

"Of course not. It's a freak show."

"I...I want to go home." Brittany turned to leave but Frank stopped her.

"Don't go. This is only the beginning. I have many more wonderful things to show you."

Brittany looked at Frank, her eyes filled with uncertainty. "I don't know how much more I can take."

"Have you ever seen a flying unicorn?" Frank asked.

"Huh?"

"Have you ever seen a flying unicorn?"

"Unicorns don't exist," Brittany protested.

"In my world they do."

Silence followed as Brittany looked curiously at Frank. "Prove it."

Frank's eyes sparkled. "The unicorn is in the next room."

Brittany forced her gaze away from the fish tank. *They look like normal fish,* she thought with a shudder, *but I know better.*

"Aren't you coming?"

Brittany nodded as she walked to the door in a stiff manner. Her head spun dizzily upon looking at the animal in the next room.

Frank gently urged Brittany through the doorway and closer to the unicorn, where it lay asleep on a soft bed of grass. It was completely white expect for its mane and tail, which were a vast array of pastel shades.

Frank knelt beside the magnificent creature. "Wake up, Bella. We have a special guest who would love to meet you."

Upon hearing Frank's voice, Bella opened her eyes, stood up and stretched her wings. Brittany marveled at Bella's piercing light blue eyes, and how white and soft her wings looked.

"You can go closer," Frank urged.

Brittany approached Bella slowly. When Bella snorted and stamped her feet, Brittany retreated in fear.

"She's a little afraid of strangers."

Brittany moved slowly towards Bella once again. With a shaky hand, she touched the unicorn's forehead. It was as silky as Brittany had imagined it to be. She frowned suddenly as her hand hit a hard bump on the unicorn's forehead. Suddenly realizing what the bump might be, Brittany swept Bella's hair to one side to reveal a small horn. The horn looked like crystal and felt just as hard.

"She's young."

"Where did you find her?" Brittany asked blissfully as she stroked Bella's back.

"In the Land of No Name."

"This can't be real. Fish can't spell and unicorns are mythical."

"They're real. You've seen them with your own eyes, Brittany. How can you not believe?"

"Because it's not real!" Brittany protested.

Bella snorted unhappily at the loud noise.

"I'll show you more," Frank said in a desperate manner. "I have bats that write mystery novels by using an inkwell and their claws as quills. I have an ant colony that has built a city and follows a strict social hierarchy. I even have a talking tree. Why can't you believe that all these things are real?"

"These things aren't suppose to be real." Brittany stopped petting Bella to look closely at Frank. "Do you really mean to tell me that there's a land with no name which is home to unbelievable creatures, and that you steal them for a freak show?"

"Yes, but my intentions aren't as bad as you make them out to be."

"How can you possibly defend your actions? If this untitled land truly exists you're no better than a common thief."

Frank looked extremely hurt by Brittany's comment. As she looked at the pain in Frank's eyes, she couldn't help but think about what he'd done for her and what he meant to her. With all that had happened in the last half an hour, Brittany had almost forgotten what she and Frank had shared.

"You'll never understand why I do the things I do."

Brittany took a deep breath and tried to muster up all the courage and trust in love she had. She reached for Frank's hand and smiled faintly. "After what I've seen I believe that anything is possible. Tell me, Frank, why you have stolen from the Land of No Name."

"I'm...I'm immortal. Do you remember me telling you that my freak show never included humans? Well, that's not exactly true. You see, I'm the main attraction of my own freak show because I never age. As for the reason why I take these magnificent creatures, it's because they need my help. I only adopt the creatures that are in danger. I also need their help, however. One needs to save money for the future, and if their future is to last forever they must be smart about earning and saving."

Brittany looked at Frank, her uncertainty fading. "If I didn't see the honesty in your eyes I would've never believed you."

"I'm glad you know me so well."

"Although I believe you, I don't understand any of this. Tell me how this all came to be."

"I used to be a freelance carpenter," Frank explained, beginning his incredible story. "I was hired to build stands for the first summer carnival in 1867.

While there, I met a very unusual man whose name was Untitled. He'd bought the largest part of the carnival's land. However, Untitled was very unhappy to find out where the location of his exhibit would be. It was located at the bottom of a steep hill, a place where he thought nobody would ever visit. He complained, but there was nothing the organizer of the carnival could do since the other locations had already been sold. Untitled finally gave up on the battle, or so everyone thought, and allowed me to build his exhibit at the bottom of the hill. After all the work was completed, I was invited to see his exhibit. Excited at the chance of seeing the freak show, I enthusiastically agreed. I thought it was so nice of Untitled to allow me to see his collection of freaks before anyone else."

Frank paused and a silence momentarily filled the tent. "I was wrong about Untitled's motives though. When I entered his exhibit he cast me into the Land of No Name. He wanted revenge on the carnival for placing his exhibit in such a poor location and he took the vengeance out on me. Untitled planned for the most evil creature in the Land of No Name to eat me. Luckily, that didn't happen since a unicorn rescued me just seconds before I could become a serpent's lunch. I made it back to the normal world, distressed, but physically all right. I fled from that carnival and never wanted to see it again. I never told anyone about what had happened. As the years passed, I started to notice that I hadn't aged. I had stayed the exact same since I was thrown into the Land of No Name."

He watched Brittany, her face a mixture of both wonder and disbelief. "My family, as well as friends who had known me for years, were very concerned. They had all aged normally except for me. Twenty years after, I still looked and felt thirty-six. I went into hiding, afraid to face the public and their suspicious gaze, and that's when I realized my condition was caused by Untitled and his actions. I also realized that I had to stop Untitled from ever trying to feed the serpents from the Land of No Name again. I went back to the carnival some fifty years later and found Untitled, exactly like he'd been many years earlier. He was terrified when he saw that I was still alive. He tried to escape, but I followed him and eventually killed him. I took over his freak show and re-named it Stanford's Freaky Shriek's Freak Show. I didn't want to own a freak show, but I knew it was the only way to stop the discovery of the entrance to the Land of No Name. You see, shortly after his murder I discovered the entrance to the mystical land. It was located beneath this very tent. I revisited the Land of No Name. While there I found many animals that were in need of my help. I adopted them and, well, you know the rest of the story."

Brittany looked at Frank with wide eyes. "I...I don't know what to say."

"I'm not sure what kind of reaction I'm looking for. I've never told anyone about this before."

"Why have you shown me all of this? Do you really trust me with such a big secret?"

"I do trust you," Frank said passionately, reaching for Brittany's hand. "I also love you. I care for you so much that I don't want to see you ever get hurt. I know what the real world is like — it's just awful! If you want, Brittany, we could live forever together. People like Mr. Watson will never hurt you again. I wouldn't let them."

"You've already proven that." Brittany looked at Frank with misty eyes. "Can I become immortal?"

"All you need to do is enter the Land of No Name. Although you could still be killed in the real world by man-made weapons, you'll never age. We would live in the real world since the Land of No Name is not much safer. They have serpents and monsters there as well."

"What does it feel like to live forever?"

"It's amazing. It's unbelievable to see how the world changes. It can get boring, but that would never be a problem again with you by my side. What do you say, Brittany, will you accept my offer?"

"It's one hell of an offer and I do care about you. I'm just not ready to give you an answer yet."

Frank looked disappointed but tried to hide it. "Take all the time you need. I do have forever, after all."

* * *

Brittany spent the next few weeks in a daze. She'd told Frank she wouldn't be at the carnival again for a while. Brittany needed time to re-adjust to normal living and decide what she wanted to do with her future. She thought living forever with Frank seemed like a dream come true. *But,* she asked herself, *would I still feel the same way in fifty years? What if Frank wasn't the incredibly sweet guy I thought he was? What if he was a crazy man who'd made up that story and was trying to lure me into some weird place where he can attack me?* Although her doubts about Frank frightened her, Brittany was convinced that he was a decent, sane man who loved her.

* * *

Brittany walked quickly to the carnival grounds. She flashed her employee card to gain access to the grounds even though she hadn't worked there for weeks. Hurrying past the numerous tents and then down the steep hill, Brittany was anxious to get to Frank. At the bottom was the large grey tent, a sight more welcoming than anything she'd ever seen before.

"Frank!" Brittany called as she entered the tent. "Are you here, Frank?"

"Brittany!" Frank emerged from another section of the tent. He ran to Brittany, embracing her. "I've been waiting for you! My worst fear was that you weren't coming back."

"I just needed time."

"I'm glad you took time for yourself. This is a huge decision, after all."

"I know. That's why I've decided not to go to the Land of No Name."

"What?" Frank asked, tears already stinging his eyes. "Why? Don't you love me?"

Brittany gave Frank a frustrated smile. "Of course I care about you. But there are other things that need to be considered. Like, can we really support ourselves forever?"

"Of course we can. I have a large sum of money in a bank account that's earning high interest. I live off the interest and have plenty more to spare. We'd be fine. Oh, Brittany, money isn't a problem. What's the real issue here?"

Brittany laughed, despite the serious topic that was being discussed. She found it incredibly funny, not to mention cute, that Frank had taken up her habit of rambling.

"I'm concerned about making such an important decision. That's why I want to wait sixteen years."

Frank looked at Brittany with newfound hope. "You mean you *do* want to come with me?"

"I do, but I want to be positive I'm making the right decision. I want to spend the next sixteen years with you. I'll be thirty-six by then – the exact same age as you. That should be enough time to make a decision I'm sure of. I'm not just waiting for my sake – I'm doing it for you as well. Because if I turn immortal and then you decide you don't love me a couple hundred years down the road, well, that's just too bad. You're stuck with me and will have to continue to provide." Brittany stuck her tongue out at Frank, indicating that although she was serious, the waiting should be fun.

"I'll never get tired of you," Frank said, wrapping his strong arms around Brittany. "Your answer makes perfect sense and is obviously the right one for both of us. I'll never stop loving you, Brittany."

"You better not because we'll be seeing *a lot* of each other over the next few years."

"And hopefully for many more years after that," Frank added, placing his lips gently upon Brittany's.

* * *

Blue Water

"This is pathetic," Lucy sighed, while sipping on a lemon iced tea. "You're pathetic," she added, pointing a perfectly manicured nail at Mandy.

"I'm not pathetic," Mandy mumbled. "I'm just shy."

"Shy?" Lucy sneered. "There are two things wrong with your reasoning, my friend. First of all, you're not shy when it comes to your job as a tourist guide for one of Hawaii's best hotels. And second, you've known Eddie and me for such a long time. You shouldn't be shy around us. Yet, I find myself being forced to sit in a crowded corner to avoid my own brother!"

"I'm not avoiding Ed," Mandy replied defensively. "I just like sitting here. If Ed happens to be at the other end of the bar, then so be it."

"I always have to ignore my brother when I'm with you," Lucy pointed out, somewhat angrily. "I'm sick of it! He's with Mr. Roberts, the most boring man in the world. It's my duty to save Eddie." Lucy quickly finished her drink and stood up. "Come on."

Mandy looked sadly into her friend's eyes. "Although Mr. Roberts may be boring, he owns a multi-million dollar cruise company. I'm just a mere employee with a half-decent job – a job which I only got because of your connections. Ed and I are nothing alike.”

Lucy stared at Mandy for a moment and then sighed. “I don’t know whether I should slap you or hug you,” she commented, sitting back down in the stool. “How long have we been friends?”

“Five years.”

“That’s a quarter of your life. You should know by now that social economic status means nothing to my family or me.”

“I know that the Curran family are the kindest millionaires to have ever walked the sands of Hawaii,” Mandy said sincerely. “Even if my poor social standing doesn’t bother you and Ed, it sure bothers me. I’m just that girl who works at Hotel Hawaii and lives in the shack across from the beach.”

“I never realized how bad your self-esteem was. Is it your silly views that keep you away from my house?”

Mandy could feel hot tears burn her eyes. She wanted to speak but knew that tears would pour down her cheeks if she opened her mouth. Mandy nodded to avoid talking.

“Maybe I can help with your self-esteem issue. I can start by saying that you have wonderful qualities. Hotel Hawaii didn’t award you with employee of the month for being a crappy person! They gave it to you because you’re so enthusiastic about your work and always go beyond the call of duty.” The smile on Lucy’s face grew wider as she continued to speak. “I can also help by inviting you to dinner at my house tonight. My whole family will be there since my father just got home from Guatemala. I’ll show you how nice us Currans can be.”

Despite the negative thoughts Mandy was entertaining in her mind, she laughed. “I know my attitude is unproductive and that it has to change. I guess that's why I told you. I wanted to put the negative feelings behind me and move on."

"Then you'll come to dinner?" Lucy asked with a hopeful smile.

"Yes."

Lucy watched Mandy as she finished her drink. She made a mental note to never call her pathetic again.

* * *

"It's really nice to have a chance to sit down and talk with you," Ed commented to Mandy, twirling spaghetti around his fork. "I feel like I know you so well. I guess that's because Lucy talks about you so much. It's hard to believe that we've never had a proper conversation before."

Mandy smiled, praying that her cheeks weren't burning as much as she felt they were. Looking at Ed, she studied his every detail with great interest. He was, in her opinion, the most handsome man she'd ever met. Ed had a muscular build that was due to his five years of training and service in the military. His face was as masculine as his body was muscular, with a strong jaw line and distinctive eyes that looked powerful, yet contradictorily gentle. Mandy had thought many times that his blue eyes were comparable to the color of the ocean when the sun shone on it.

Mandy turned her gaze away from Ed and to the plate of spaghetti in front of her. "It's nice to be here," she began to say. However, her words were cut short by the grumbling voice of Mr. Curran.

"Yes, it's nice to have you here, Mandy," Mr. Curran agreed with less enthusiasm than Ed had displayed. "I don't understand why you chose to come over for dinner on this particular night though."

Mandy felt her cheeks burn with even more vigor. Although Mr. Curran's words were spoken quickly and quietly, she had heard everything. Unfortunately for Mandy and Mr. Curran, Mrs. Curran had heard her husband's words as well.

"Matthew!" Mrs. Curran exclaimed. "What did you just say? I'm sure I misheard you."

Mr. Curran looked around the table with a guilty expression on his face. He knew he was cornered. "Mandy could've picked a better time to come over for dinner. I'm just back from Guatemala. It would be nice to have a bit of peace and quiet."

"Dad!" Lucy cried angrily. "What's gotten into you?"

"I'm tired!" Mr. Curran yelled, standing up and slamming his fork on the table. "You really shouldn't expect me to put on some fake persona for every dinner guest we have. I've had enough damn schmoozing in Guatemala to last me a lifetime. And do you know where my schmoozing gets me? Nowhere! My so-called partners in Guatemala have just informed me that they're not reinstating the contract which provides twenty-five percent of this family's income. That's right – the workers in Guatemala have gotten a better offer from another shoe company!"

"You can't blame the Guatemalan people for looking out for their own needs first," Lucy pointed out. Although Lucy believed in what she was saying, she was only voicing her opinion to take the embarrassment away from Mandy. She hated to think how awful Mandy must be feeling.

The room became silent as Mr. Curran stormed out. The only sound came from the slamming of the door.

"I...I have to go," Mandy stuttered.

"I'll walk you to the door," Lucy and Ed said sympathetically at the exact same moment.

"That's...that's not necessary," Mandy stuttered again as she ran towards the door and then let herself out in a hurry. Once she was out of the house, she leaned against the door and breathed heavily. She was trying desperately to hold back the tears which threatened to pour down her face at any moment.

As she ran from the Curran's mansion and back to her shack on the beach, Mandy recalled the event that had just occurred and the words that had been spoken. She was certain that it was the most humiliating moment of her entire life.

* * *

Mandy woke up early the next morning. The sun was just rising over the blue ocean as she made herself breakfast. She hadn't slept well; she kept having nightmares about the degrading experience at the Curran's house the night before. What made Mandy all the more furious was that after the incident Lucy hadn't called her. Worried, she wondered if Lucy no longer wanted to be her friend.

Mandy quickly changed into her swimsuit and grabbed a towel. She tried to shake the negative thoughts from her head as she headed towards the sound of the pounding waves.

There weren't many people at the beach; just a few surf fanatics.

Mandy placed her blue and purple beach towel on the clean yellow sand and proceeded to watch as the surfers rode the waves. Her eyes were immediately fixated upon Steven Furlong and his younger sister Jacki. Mandy had known Steven for three years since they both worked at Hotel Hawaii. Although she knew a lot about him, they hardly talked. As the son of the hotel's manager of recreation, his official position was termed as "co-manager of recreation". It was much more distinguished than her "tourist guide" label.

But now, as Mandy watched Steven proudly instruct his sister on how to handle a wave, she felt no difference between them. They were both sun-loving individuals who wanted to have a good time. That was one of the reasons why Mandy loved the beach so much; it was the only place where she felt at par with everyone else.

He's cute, Mandy thought as she watched Steven easily ride a wave. *And kind,* she added, noticing how he helped his sister onto the surfboard. Mandy smiled as Jacki rode a small wave without falling off the surfboard. She watched as Steven slapped his sister a high five and then ruffled her hair with his hand. *He seems like the perfect guy,* she thought. *But I've only got eyes for Ed.* Mandy sighed as she lay back on her towel.

Mandy was readjusting her sunglasses when she heard a shrill scream. She immediately jumped to her feet. Focusing her attention on the direction of the sound, Mandy gasped in horror at what she saw. Steven was struggling out of the water with his screaming sister at his side. He seemed to be dragging her onto the sand in a fury. Although seeing Jacki in such a terrified state was shocking, Mandy's eyes were more focused on the surfboard that had washed onto the shore. The once stylish, yellow surfboard was broken in half; one of the ends had the imprint of shark teeth.

"Oh no!" Mandy gasped as she hurried towards the crowd that had already formed around Steven and Jacki.

"What happened?" Mandy heard a man ask.

"Is she all right?" another person asked.

"Get out of my way!" a lifeguard yelled as he maneuvered through the crowd.

Mandy couldn't hear much over the sound of the waves crashing against the shoreline and the concerned mutters from the bystanders. Amid the noise, words such as "shark", "screaming" and "panic" filtered through her ears, tightening her chest with fear. She overheard the phrase "out of nowhere" and it immediately sickened her.

Minutes fluttered away in what seemed like seconds. Soon, an ambulance had arrived at the beach. Mandy watched from a distance as two paramedics transferred Jacki onto a stretcher and then took her away in the ambulance. A shaken-up Steven was at his sister's side with every step the workers took.

Mandy looked at the ground where Jacki had been just moments ago. The sand was wet. She was relieved to see that the dark sand was soaking with water and not blood.

* * *

Knock. Knock. Knock
Mandy looked up from the small stove where she was stirring a saucepan filled with her dinner. Heading towards the door, she wondered who it was. Mandy knew who she hoped it was – Lucy. She still

hadn't heard from her since that horrible dining experience one night ago.

"Ed! What are you doing here?" Mandy exclaimed after opening the door.

"I'm sorry that I've come over unannounced. May I come in?"

"Of course," Mandy mumbled in embarrassment, opening the door wider and stepping backwards. She didn't mean to be impolite; she was just shocked at Ed's presence. He had never visited her before.

"I just want to apologize. My father has never acted so rude before. His behavior was so uncharacteristic that we were somewhat relieved to discover it really wasn't him."

"Huh? That man wasn't your real father? Who was he then?"

Ed couldn't resist the urge to laugh. "Technically, he *is* my father. What I meant to say is that he's ill. While in Guatemala he caught a virus he wasn't vaccinated against. This virus, along with the stress of losing the contract, caused his irrational behavior. He's at the hospital right now."

"Oh my gosh! Is he all right?"

"Yes. He'll be back to his normal self within a few days. He's been given the antidote and only needs rest now. I promise you that my father will apologize as soon as he feels better."

"That's not necessary. I'm relieved he didn't mean what he said. I'm just sorry that it happened at all – with him getting sick in the first place, I mean."

"All the apologies are directed towards you, Mandy," Ed said sincerely. "And I promise that they'll be delivered."

Mandy smiled gratefully. "Thanks for letting me know what's going on."

"Lucy would've told you herself but she's taken on the stereotypical female role and is catering to my father's every whim."

Mandy felt relieved to hear that Lucy hadn't ditched her. With the Lucy situation no longer encompassing her thoughts, she focused on other things; namely, the fact that Ed was standing just inches away from her.

"Do you like women who take on the stereotypical role?"

"Not at all," Ed replied quickly. "I may be an old-fashioned type of man but I do believe in equality."

Mandy tried to hide the smile that had begun to play upon her lips. Ed's answer couldn't have been more perfect. She felt her cheeks burn red and her tongue tie in a knot. It was as if every sensible thought Mandy had ever had just slipped her mind. Thankfully, she didn't have to say anything.

"While I'm here," Ed began, his own face growing a bit red, "I should ask you something."

"You should?" Mandy asked breathlessly.

"Yeah. Would you like to help me on the Blue Oceana tomorrow? Lucy usually helps me, but she'll still be busy looking after our father. You actually don't have to do much. You can even just watch the waves go by, if you like."

Ed's nervousness made Mandy feel more confident and at ease with the whole situation. "I wouldn't be much help if all I did was watch the waves," Mandy pointed out with a smile.

"Yeah, well."

"I'd love to come," Mandy said quickly, not wanting Ed to think she was being rude.

"That's great. Would you like me to pick you up in the morning?"

"Or I could meet you at the docks," Mandy suggested. "I live just five minutes away. When should I meet you there?"

"9:30 would be good. I have a tour booked for 10:10."

"Sounds good."

Silence seemed to echo around the shack as Mandy and Ed tried to think of something to say.

"I'll see you tomorrow then."

"See you tomorrow," Ed replied as he left Mandy's shack. "Thanks for helping me out," he added, turning around suddenly. "I really appreciate it."

Mandy smiled happily as she watched Ed walk away. She had to gather all her strength to resist the urge to jump around in joy.

* * *

Mandy arrived at the dock, which housed the Blue Oceana, at 9:25 the next morning. It was a beautiful day for a cruise. The sun was shining upon the ocean, white clouds littered the light blue sky, and the boat swayed over the waves as they crashed against the dock and bounced back. The boat had three levels which were all simply, yet beautifully, decorated. The Blue Oceana was mostly white with blue seats and the occasional stripe of colored paint over the exterior.

Ready and eager to get on-board, ticket holders were wandering around the harbor and commenting on how beautiful the Blue Oceana looked. Those who hadn't purchased their ticket beforehand were waiting in a long queue.

Mandy felt important as she walked by the passengers.

"Hi, Mandy," Ed greeted her. "I'm glad you're here."

"I said I'd come. I always keep my word." Although Mandy's exterior was calm and collected, inside she was a jumble of emotions. She thought Ed looked absolutely gorgeous. He was wearing a casual pair of dark blue slacks and a white polo shirt. His outfit was completed with a pair of dark sunglasses.

"So, what can I help you with?" Mandy asked.

Ed offered Mandy his hand to help her over the bump in between the stairs to the boat and the boat itself. Mandy appreciatively took Ed's hand, although she was perfectly capable of boarding the boat herself.

"Well," Ed muttered as if he were only now thinking up Mandy's task. "You could stamp the tickets of the passengers who board the boat."

"Sounds like fun," Mandy replied, taking the stamping device that Ed handed to her.

"The passengers are allowed to start boarding the boat now." Ed walked to a nearby pole which held a large microphone and picked it up. "Boarding of the Blue Oceana will start now. Please line up and have your ticket ready. Thank you."

Mandy giggled like a twelve-year-old as Ed winked at her. She smiled as she stamped the tickets which the people handed to her. When the last person had boarded, Ed led Mandy towards the front of the boat.

"We'll be taking off in just a few minutes, folks," Ed announced loudly.

Mandy couldn't help but laugh out loud.

"What's so funny?"

"Your use of the word "folks" is funny. It's not a word one would expect to hear on a million dollar boat."

"You don't know me very well then," Ed commented, sounding a bit annoyed. "Just because I'm the captain of a boat and come from a well-off family doesn't mean I'm a complete snob. I may be a little bit of a snob, but definitely not a complete one!" Ed laughed, indicating that he wasn't offended.

"You're not a snob," Mandy assured him with a half smile, looking deep into his eyes.

"You'll surely classify me as a snob when I say what I'm about to say."

"Just say it."

"This boat is actually worth 6 million dollars — not that million you were talking about." Suddenly, he leaned forward and kissed Mandy on the cheek.

Mandy gasped. Her mind as well as her heart was racing. "What was that for?"

"For helping me out," Ed said, looking a little bit embarrassed. He cleared his throat and then started the boat.

Mandy had trouble concentrating as Ed explained what each button and device on the boat was; she was too giddy with happiness.

"You know a lot about the ocean," Mandy commented, after Ed had talked non-stop about it for half an hour.

"It's just one of my many passions. Sorry if I bored you. I can get carried away very easily when the topic of discussion comes to the ocean and boats."

"Then you won't mind if I ask you about something that happened yesterday at the beach?"

"Of course not," Ed replied, adjusting course by turning the wheel of the boat slightly. "I presume you're talking about the shark attack?"

"Yes. What happened exactly?"

"Well, I'm not too sure how accurate my information is. My mother was the one who told me about it. She heard the story from another woman who is a friend of the victim's mother. Like I said, the grapevine of information is quite long. I would hate to tell you something that was incorrect."

"Tell me already!"

"From what I've heard, a young girl, Jacki Furlong, was surfing with her brother when a hammerhead shark attacked. The shark ruined her surfboard but, thankfully, she's all right. Jacki was released from the hospital this morning. She was being treated for shock."

"I'm so glad to hear that Jacki's okay."

"Do you know her?"

"Yes. I work with her brother. I was also there when the shark attack happened."

"You weren't in the water, were you?" Ed asked frightfully.

"No. Aren't hammerhead sharks really dangerous?"

"Extremely. I don't know how the coastguards confirmed the breed of the shark, but if it really was a hammerhead shark Jacki is one hell of a lucky girl."

"My thoughts exactly," Mandy muttered, more to herself than Ed. "How in the world did Jacki survive an attack from a hammerhead shark?"

"I don't know, but I'm glad she's all right."

"Me too," Mandy said with a shiver.

"You said you worked with Jacki's brother?"

"Yes. We both work together at Hotel Hawaii."

"What do you do there?" Ed asked, genuinely interested.

"I'm a tourist guide."

"It's funny that Lucy always talks about you but never mentions what your life is like."

"What do you mean?"

"Well," Ed began, "I know that you and Lucy always hang out at the beach. Unfortunately, my knowledge ends there. I'd like to know more about you."

"Why?" Mandy always hated it when the topic of her lifestyle was brought up during a conversation.

"You seem like a really interesting person," Ed said, a blush filling his cheeks. "Perhaps, you'd like to go out with me some time?"

Mandy didn't answer Ed's question right away. Although her heart was screaming "yes", her bashfulness was screaming "no". She *really* didn't want to discuss her personal life with him. Mandy knew that Ed wouldn't like her if he knew what she was really like.

"Um, Mandy, did you hear my question?"

Mandy looked at Ed's hopeful, hot face. She felt angry at herself for even considering *not* taking Ed up on his offer. "I heard your question and I'd love to go out with you."

"Great! I have tomorrow off since the Blue Oceana only operates every other day and on weekends. Is there any place special you would like to go? How about the Sandbar restaurant on Fifth Avenue? They have the best lobster dinner in Hawaii."

Mandy bit her lip. She'd never been to the Sandbar restaurant before, but she had heard that it was very expensive. If Ed expected them to go Dutch, Mandy would only be able to afford a glass of water – assuming that was complimentary.

"That sounds nice," Mandy lied. "But is there any place less expensive?"

Ed's face colored slightly. "I'm paying for the meal, of course. It's a date. *I* asked *you*."

Mandy sighed. Their social economic status had already interfered with their relationship. If Ed weren't so cute and related to Lucy, she would've probably called the whole date off.

"I'd love to spend the day at the beach with you," Mandy admitted. "You could even buy me a hot dog from the local vendor," she added with a playful smile.

"That does sound like more fun than a restaurant." The concept of *not* spending a lot of money on a date was new for Ed. He'd gone out with a few girls who had come from wealthy families. They had always expected him to spend over a hundred dollars on a meal. Needless to say, those relationships never lasted long.

"What time do you want to go to the beach?" Ed inquired.

"Does eleven o'clock sound okay?"

"Sounds great, but there's one thing I refuse to do while at the beach."

"Go swimming?" Mandy asked with raised eyebrows.

Ed nodded. "If that hammerhead shark is still roaming these waters there's no way I'm fully emerging myself in the ocean. I may dip my toe in the water's edge, but that's all!"

"Don't worry. There's no way I'm going in the ocean either."

Mandy shivered as Ed turned the boat around. She couldn't get the sound of Jacki's scream and the image of her helpless body out of her head.

* * *

Mandy glanced at the clock that hung on her wall; it read 10:54. She turned her attention back to the mirror and continued to apply eyeliner. She smiled at the face staring back at her. If there was one thing Mandy felt good about, it was her appearance. She had an athletic build and stood tall at five foot eight. Her skin was well-tanned and glossy from all the time she spent in the sun. Mandy considered her hair and eyes to be her best features. Her hair went past her shoulders and was a magnificent mix of red and brown. A stunning mix of blue and green, her eyes were as spectacular as her hair. They always twinkled when something interesting or fun was about to happen. Right now, Mandy's eyes were twinkling and shining with so much vigor that she was afraid Ed would be blinded if he looked into them. She giggled at the thought.

Knock. Knock. Knock.

Mandy took one last look at herself in the mirror and, satisfied, headed towards the door.

"Hey!"

"Hi," Ed replied as he kissed Mandy on the cheek. "You look very beautiful."

"Thanks. You don't look so bad yourself." Mandy looked Ed up and down. His body was so muscular and tanned that Mandy was afraid she'd start to drool. Ed wore a white muscle tee and blue shorts; he looked like a professional basketball player.

"Are you ready for our day at the beach?"

Mandy nodded happily. She loved how Ed personalized the day by naming it "our". She grabbed her beach bag and closed the door to her shack.

Together, Mandy and Ed headed towards the sparkling blue water and yellow sand.

There were few people on the beach. Even the number of dedicated surfers had declined greatly. Mandy had picked up a copy of the newspaper while in town that morning to find that the news about the hammerhead attack on the thirteen-year-old girl had circulated around the shores of Hawaii. Local newspapers had published the facts of Jacki's survival just as Ed had described. Jacki was, miraculously, doing fine.

"At least we don't have to fight for a space on the beach," Ed commented, placing his large towel under a palm tree.

Mandy placed her own towel next to Ed's. They settled comfortably onto the sand, and watched as the waves crashed against the shore.

"It really is beautiful here," Ed murmured peacefully. "You're lucky to live so close to the beach."

"Me? Lucky?"

"Yes," Ed replied firmly.

"No one has ever called me lucky before."

"Then they haven't seen you in the way I have," Ed said, turning his gaze towards Mandy.

"You hardly know me," Mandy said quietly and almost sadly.

"Then tell me. Let me know who the real Mandy Landon is."

"Are you sure you want to know? It might change your perspective of me."

"It will do that," he agreed. "It'll make me like you even more."

Mandy blushed at Ed's comment. "All right," she took a deep breath. "I was born in Hawaii. I used to live in a small, but nice, house on the inland. My parents didn't have a lot of money but they had enough to maintain a happy lifestyle. When I was only five years old, my parents went to visit another

Hawaiian island. My father, who worked as the supervisor of a company that packaged and exported coconuts, was transferred to another island. Therefore, my parents were looking for property there. They left me at home with my grandmother and never came back. I found out later that they were in an airplane accident. There were no survivors."

As Mandy paused to take a deep breath, Ed cast her a sympathetic gaze.

"I lived with my grandmother in that shack," Mandy continued. "She died seven years ago. When I met Lucy I was working at Papa's Bar and Grill as a bartender. Lucy and I immediately hit it off and became close friends. She was the one who got me the job with Hotel Hawaii." Self-conscious of her past, Mandy focused her gaze on a distant lighthouse, unable to meet Ed's eyes.

After a few minutes of silence, Ed spoke. "Whoa. It sounds like you've had a very hard life. You should be very proud of all you've accomplished. The odds may have been against you, but you've definitely overcome them."

"Do you really mean that or do you just feel sorry for me?"

Ed became very quiet as he looked intensely at Mandy. "I do feel something for you but I guarantee it's not pity." He leaned in closer and kissed her gently on the lips. Suddenly, he pulled away. "I'm sorry if I overstepped any boundaries. I've just wanted to do that for so long. I really didn't mean to take advantage of the situation. I just..."

"You talk too much." Mandy pulled Ed closer. She wrapped her arms around his strong body and pulled her lips to his.

"I'm so glad you feel the way I do," Ed said when they finally broke apart.

"Of course I do." Mandy snuggled into his chest.

"I have a surprise for you. How would you like a private tour on The Swordfish?"

"The Swordfish?"

"It's a boat that my family owns. Although much smaller than the Blue Oceana, it's still a reasonably sized boat. It can hold fifty-five people."

"It sounds great! Can we go now?"

"I knew you'd like my idea," Ed said through a laugh. "You seemed to have a lot of fun on the Blue Oceana yesterday."

"I did." Mandy quickly stood up.

"I can tell that you're anxious to go. Maybe we should just rest on the beach for a little bit longer." Ed leaned back on the large towel and closed his eyes.

Mandy felt herself getting annoyed until he opened his eyes and stood up.

"Or we can go now," Ed said with a smile.

It only took ten minutes to get to the docks. Soon, Mandy and Ed were on the purple and white boat, heading out to the ocean.

"The ocean is so beautiful," Mandy gushed, while looking upon the crystal clear water.

"I agree." Ed put the boat's gear into neutral and joined Mandy.

Everything seemed so quiet and peaceful as he slipped his arm around Mandy's waist and pulled her closer to him. She giggled, but willingly stepped closer to him. Their lips were about to meet when the boat suddenly surged forward.

Mandy had been standing next to the boat's railing a second ago; now she was half way over it. She let out a scream as she felt herself going overboard. All Mandy could see was the light colored water rocking furiously and her shadow being cast upon it.

Shocked and frozen in fear, Ed had never felt the boat shake so fiercely. He quickly got over the surprise as he reached for Mandy. As he grabbed the back of her t-shirt and prepared to pull her back, another bump against the boat made him lose his grip.

"Damn!" Ed grunted as another blow from the side of the boat made him tumble forward and then fall backwards. He bashed into the wall and then landed hard on the boat's floor. The fire extinguisher, which was hanging on the wall, fell from its latch and hit his head. He groaned from the sharp pain that traveled throughout his body. Nevertheless, he shakily got back on his feet and staggered towards Mandy.

Mandy cringed as the boat was bumped harshly for the third time. She could hear a lot of noise from behind her, but couldn't figure out what it was.

"Hold on!" Ed tried to reach Mandy. However, the sudden and fierce bumps tossed him back to the floor.

Mandy clutched onto the boat's railing, but the bumps and waves were too violent.

"Mandy!" Ed yelled.

Mandy fell overboard, her shrill scream rising over the crashing waves.

The boat continued to shake as Ed crawled to the edge. Using all his strength, he grasped the edge of the boat and peered overboard. He almost choked on his fear at what he saw.

The water vibrated harshly as the silhouette of a large shark swam from underneath the boat. Ed instantly recognized it as a hammerhead shark.

"Get out of the water!" Ed screamed.

I'm going to drown, Mandy thought, feeling the strength of the current. She could see The Swordfish bouncing up and down, but she couldn't see Ed. She was about to call for help but stopped when she saw a dark shadow approach her. *Oh my...* Mandy thought as she realized that the shadow was a shark. She tried to swim but it was useless. Mandy could hardly tread water in these conditions, far less swim in them. She began to shake as she thought about her impending doom.

The hammerhead shark swam closer to Mandy and splashed its tail, causing even more waves. Then it began to circle her.

Although the boat was rocking, Ed finally managed to get on his feet. He ran shakily to the side of the boat and opened the box marked "emergency". Ed searched through the box in a fury and then grabbed a long rope. He ran back to the edge of the boat and, leaning over, let out an earth-shattering cry. The shark had tightened the circle around Mandy and was going in for the kill. Ed threw the rope into the water, praying that it would either distract the shark or benefit Mandy. He was in so much physical and emotional pain that he was no longer thinking straight.

Despite the salty water splashing in her eyes, Mandy could see the shark's dark outline coming towards her. Trying to stay as still as possible, she prayed that the shark would bypass her. Mandy began to sink in the water but she didn't dare move.

Suddenly, the hammerhead shark turned around and snapped at something else in the water.

"Grab the rope!" Ed yelled, watching as the shark whirled away from Mandy and began to chase a fast moving object.

Ed's voice snapped Mandy back to reality. Swimming in the choppy water, she made her way towards the rope. Within a few minutes, she grasped onto the lifeline with trembling hands. Ed began pulling her in and didn't stop until she was back on the boat.

"Oh my gosh!" Mandy said breathlessly, flinging herself into Ed's arms. "What just happened?"

"I don't know." Sweat was running down Ed's forehead. He held onto Mandy tightly, thanking whoever was responsible for her survival. Ed closed his eyes and tried to calm the beating of his heart.

Mandy pulled herself from Ed's grasp and turned towards the ocean. Her eyes widened as she stared at the vibrating water. The hammerhead shark and its new prey were making the water even choppier. She planted her feet firmly on the deck as she leaned over the boat and tried to get a better look at the moving objects in the water.

"Get back from the edge!" Ed grabbed Mandy. His hands had just wrapped around Mandy's waist when he saw what had startled her. Ed loosened his grip as he stared at what had distracted the hammer-head shark and saved Mandy's life.

"It's a person," Mandy realized in horror.

"It's not a person."

"Yes, it is!" Mandy reached for the rope that had saved her. She threw it into the water and screamed at the person who was being chased by the shark. "Grab the rope!"

Ed tightened his grip on Mandy's waist once again and then pulled her back. She let out a cry of protest, but allowed him to take her to safety. Mandy did, however, hold onto the rope tightly.

"We have to save him," Mandy begged Ed. "He saved my life. We can't just leave him in the water with the shark!"

"Mandy, that wasn't a human. It was swimming too fast."

"You're wrong!" Tears flowed down Mandy's face.

"Mandy! I'm not!"

"What is it then?"

"I don't know," Ed admitted shakily. "But we have to get out of here." The boat was beginning to rock fiercely once again. Whatever was in the water with the hammerhead shark was certainly putting up a tough fight.

"No! You didn't see the person as closely as I did. I know what I saw, Ed."

"Stay here," Ed instructed, giving into Mandy's pleas.

Ed crept close to the boat's edge and looked over. The hammerhead shark and the mystery object were only a few feet away. As he looked closer, he let out a low gasp. The hammerhead wasn't chasing the thing that had saved Mandy; instead, they were fighting. He couldn't see the fight well because of the rushing water; however, he was relatively certain he saw the body of a man. Ed wasn't sure what to do. He knew there was no way that a man could fight a hammerhead shark, for the period of time he had, and still be alive.

"What do you see?"

"I don't know." Ed ran back to the emergency box and lifted out a lifesaving ring.

"Is it a man?" Mandy cried in terror as she tried to reach Ed's side. Her attempt was in vain as she fell to the floor.

"Stay where you are. If there's a person out there, I'll get him back safely."

Ed carefully reached the boat's edge and threw the life saving ring into the water. He held onto the rope attached to it and hoped for the best. Ed waited and waited, listening to the crashing waves against the boat. He was flabbergasted that the fight was lasting so long.

Ed was in so much pain and emotional confusion that he was surprised when he felt a tug on the rope. Fighting his way back to reality, he pulled on the rope. The waves lessened, producing nothing more than an aftermath of gentle currents.

A sweat began to break out on Ed's forehead as he continued to pull in the object on the ring. "Help me pull the rope!"

Mandy hurried over to Ed, grabbed part of the rope and began to pull. Ed neared the boat's edge, but continued to apply his strength to the rope. He looked over the edge and then let out a startled cry. A man with long blonde hair was holding onto the ring. He was almost out of the water.

"Keep pulling," Ed instructed, backing away from the edge and joining Mandy.

Together, they pulled until the man was in the boat. Then, in perfect unison, they let out a loud scream. Ed and Mandy hadn't pulled a man onto their boat; they had saved something that was half-man, half-fish.

The strange creature flopped on the deck. It tried to lift itself up but fell back onto the boat's floor.

"Stay back," Ed demanded as Mandy moved forward. He looked at the creature in bewilderment. The top half of the thing was a normal-looking man. However, the rest of him was just a sparkly blue fish tail.

"He needs help." Mandy harbored a deep appreciation for this creature. Although it was certainly creepy, it *had* saved her life. She knelt beside the creature and stared at it, amazed at its beauty. The top half of the man was completely normal, except for the fish fins that were on both of his arms. As

Mandy stared at the unidentified entity it suddenly occurred to her what it was.

Mandy looked at Ed, her eyes wide with wonder. "Do you know what this is?"

"No. Is it even a man?"

"Yes," Mandy replied, while looking at the scratches and cuts that covered its body. "It's a merman."

Ed looked at Mandy with bulging eyes. "I don't doubt anything now," he confessed, approaching the merman. "He's badly hurt." Ed pointed to the merman's arms and chest. "He needs medical attention."

"Are you all right?" Mandy asked the merman.

The merman lay still on the ground. His eyes were closed and he was breathing heavily.

"He looks like he's in a lot of pain. Maybe we should…"

"He's stopped breathing!" Mandy cut Ed off and gestured wildly towards the merman's still, silent chest. She immediately jumped into action and began performing CPR.

Ed watched in amazement as his new girlfriend changed into an emergency medical technician. If someone were to tell him what this day would entail, he wouldn't have believed it. Although he hoped Mandy's CPR efforts would revive the merman, he was more concerned about her catching a weird disease. Ed felt like being sick as he watched Mandy perform mouth-to-mouth.

"He's coming around." Mandy was so relieved when the merman coughed up water and opened his eyes. She was getting dizzy; performing CPR much longer would've been out of the question.

"Thank you," the merman said breathlessly. He looked at his fish tail and flapped it up and down a few times. Then he looked at his arms and flexed them. The fins on his arms rose up and down as he moved. The merman sighed in relief when he realized he was okay.

Mandy stared at the merman. His face was very handsome. His piercing blue eyes complimented his long blonde hair. Two dimples appeared as his lips spread into a smile.

"I should be thanking you," Mandy finally spoke. "You saved my life back there. Thank you for distracting that hammerhead shark."

"No. You saved my life."

"Then we're even," Mandy replied. "He also helped," she added, pointing her index finger towards Ed.

As the merman looked at him, Ed held up his hand and wiggled his fingers in a greeting. He didn't know what else to do or what to say. It wasn't everyday that he met a merman.

"You saved Jacki, didn't you?" Mandy asked the merman.

"Jacki?"

"The girl who was attacked by the hammerhead shark a few days ago. You saved her, right?"

The merman shook his head. "That wasn't me. It must've been another merman."

"Another merman?" Ed exclaimed, jumping into the conversation. "There are more like you?"

"Of course. There are many."

"Why hasn't anyone found you before?" Ed demanded.

"We stay hidden."

"You need to rest," Mandy interrupted. "You must've exhausted yourself from the fight with the hammerhead."

"I would hardly call that a fight. I was just trying to survive."

"Well, you did survive and you also managed to save my life. In my eyes that makes you a hero."

Ed's mouth dropped open upon hearing Mandy's praise for the merman. *Is she hitting on him?* Now he really did feel like being sick.

"Do we have any antiseptic to put on his cuts?" Mandy asked Ed.

"No," the merman said quickly. "Don't touch my wounds with human medicine. My wounds will only heal with the power of Algae Skin."

"What's Algae Skin?"

"It's the formula that heals a merman and mermaid's every wound. It's what our ancestors used to create us."

"Create you?" Ed practically yelled. "How do you create mermen and mermaids?"

"I can't say. I've already spoken too much." The merman suddenly turned towards Mandy. "Thank you for saving me, but I must go now."

"You can't leave! There's so much I want to know about you."

"I can't stay in your world. My ancestors tried to do so before but it failed."

The merman cast Mandy a sad glance and then stood up. Mandy and Ed were amazed to see his blue tail fold back and become like two feet which were stuck together. The merman walked without difficulty but then fell suddenly.

"Are you all right?" Mandy asked, running to the merman's side.

"I'm tired."

"You can't swim like this. If the shark comes back you'll easily be defeated."

"I suppose you're right. I'll rest and then go home."

As Mandy and Ed helped the merman onto a cot they both wondered where the merman's home was.

The merman slept soundly and didn't wake up until two hours later. During that time, Mandy and Ed talked non-stop about Mandy's near death experience and the discovery of the merman.

"So, where do you think the other mermen and mermaids are?" Mandy asked Ed in between sips from a bottle of water.

"I have no clue." Ed smiled at Mandy, no longer jealous of her attention towards the merman. *After all,* he reasoned with himself, *it would be weird if someone wasn't impressed by the discovery of a mythical creature.*

"Why do you want to know where my kind dwell?" The merman had seemingly appeared out of nowhere. "Do you want to know so you can tell the whole world and then destroy us?"

"Of course not!" Mandy looked at the angry merman. "We're just curious. Everyone thinks mermen and mermaids aren't real."

"Good. That's how my ancestors planned it."

"I'm sorry if we offended you. We're just so amazed by seeing you."

The merman sighed, his disposition turning from anger to compassion. "You saved my life. I owe you the truth."

Mandy bit her lip. She deferred from reminding the merman that he'd been the one to save her first. "We're listening."

"It all started over a thousand years ago when mermen and mermaids were first invented."

"Invented?" Ed questioned. "You were invented?"

"Shhh…" Mandy scolded Ed. "Let the merman speak."

The merman nodded. "Mermen and mermaids were invented by two humans."

Mandy and Ed looked expectantly at the merman when he stopped talking.

"What's wrong?" Mandy asked finally.

"We shouldn't be talking."

"Why not?"

"Because you don't know my name and I don't know yours. It's a tradition for mermen and mermaids to introduce themselves before they talk."

Mandy had to bite her lip again. She repressed the urge to say that one must speak to introduce themselves.

"My name is Mandy Landon."

"I'm Ed Curran."

"I'm Blue Oceana," the merman said proudly.

"Excuse me?" Ed blurted out. "That can't be your name – that's the name of my family's boat!"

"I know. I'm named after your boat. Before my mother was made into a mermaid, she used to travel on the Blue Oceana weekly. She loved that boat and misses it very much. My mother even watches the Blue Oceana from the water sometimes. She says you're an excellent captain, by the way."

"This is unreal!" Ed cried, not sure whether he was delighted or terrified. "You know how to turn people into mermen and mermaids? And your mother used to be a human? This can't be happening!"

"Oh, I assure you it is. It's been happening for years. Since a mermaid can only have one child in her lifetime and since that child is usually a male, we must turn female humans into mermaids."

"But how can someone turn into a mythical creature?" Mandy muttered, more to herself than Blue Oceana.

"Perhaps I should start from the beginning. Over a thousand years ago there were two scientists named Merman and Mermaid Ocean. They were different from the other scientists who studied how to cure human ailments. Mr. and Mrs. Ocean wanted to create a superior human that was invincible and could live in water as well as land. Through the injection of fish DNA into a human body they created something that was half-human and half-fish. Merman and Mermaid classified their newly invented species after themselves. Although they had created a complex creature, Mr. and Mrs. Ocean couldn't make them invincible. The mortality of the mermen and mermaids became a problem as they were hunted down. People in society didn't like anyone who was different."

"That's awful," Mandy said, suddenly understanding the mythical creature's pain.

Blue Oceana continued with sadness in his eyes. "After they killed many mermen and mermaids, the people of this very country came after Mr. and Mrs. Ocean. With nowhere to run, Mr. and Mrs. Ocean injected themselves with their own formula, Algae Skin, and then fled to the water. They joined the other mermen and mermaids that had managed to survive and lived in the underwater caverns until they died. The formula for Algae Skin was not lost along with Mr. and Mrs. Ocean's death though. The scientists taught the other mermen and mermaids how to transform humans into these magnificent creatures. A few years after Mr. and Mrs. Ocean's death, the mermen and mermaids decided to come out of their underwater cave and back to dry land. Once again met with hostility, they were driven back to the ocean and have stayed there ever since." Blue Oceana paused to look sadly at Mandy and Ed.

"That's why mermen and mermaids are so afraid of humans. We all grew up hearing the horrible stories of our ancestors' brutal murder."

"Wait a minute," Ed said suspiciously. "You said mermen and mermaids haven't emerged from the water since their second attempt to fit in with humans. Yet, you also said your kind creates mermen and mermaids with Algae Skin. Your two statements are contradictory." Ed crossed his arms as he waited for Blue Oceana to explain.

"There are exceptions to every story. In order for our species to survive we *must* recruit women."

"If you're feeling better maybe you should go now." Mandy backed up. She didn't like the way Blue Oceana was looking at her.

"I can't." Blue Oceana moved closer to Mandy. "I've told you too much. You need to come with me."

"Don't take another step." Ed stood in between Blue Oceana and Mandy.

"Get out of the way. This doesn't involve you."

"Of course it does. I know just as much as Mandy does. You can't take her without taking me."

"We don't need mermen — we need mermaids. And that's what you're going to become, my sweet Mandy."

Mandy whimpered and hid behind Ed. She couldn't believe what was happening to her. She also couldn't believe how Blue Oceana was so nice one minute and then evil the next.

"Let me rephrase myself," Ed said harshly, moving closer to Blue Oceana. "What I meant to say is that you won't be taking her or me."

"I regret to inform you that she *is* coming with me." Blue Oceana jumped high in the air and grabbed Mandy. Within seconds, Blue Oceana was swimming away with Mandy in tow.

"Mandy!" Ed screamed, looking at the ocean with fierce anger. He ran to the boat's engine and revved it up. Pulling the throttle towards him, he sped after Mandy and Blue Oceana.

"Let me go!" Water splashed in Mandy's mouth as Blue Oceana swam up and down in the water. His grip was so tight that she felt as if she was going to break in half. Blue Oceana refused to listen to Mandy as he swam faster. "Why are you doing this? Why would you save me only to kill me?"

"I'm not going to kill you." Blue Oceana slowed his pace. "I would never kill you! You're so beautiful – the most beautiful woman I've ever seen. You can be my mermaid. Oh, it'll be wonderful. You'll make such a pretty mermaid bride!"

Mandy felt herself shake. Not only was she afraid by Blue Oceana's words, she was also afraid of his tone of voice. His words were coming out in a shaky, slurred tone. He sounded completely different from the half-man, half-fish Mandy had known just a couple of hours ago.

"What's that noise?" Blue Oceana snapped suddenly.

Mandy heard the noise also. She turned her head to see The Swordfish coming full speed towards them. "Move!" Mandy yelled as Blue Oceana failed to swim away from the boat. She looked at The Swordfish and then Blue Oceana with wide eyes. Blue Oceana looked as if he were in shock. Taking advantage of the situation, Mandy tried to escape from his grasp. Her sudden movements alerted Blue Oceana and immediately he was snapped out of his trance. He began to swim away with Mandy in his grasp. It was too late. She closed her eyes and waited to die.

Suddenly, she felt herself being thrown to the side. Her eyes fluttered open to see The Swordfish slide past her with just inches to spare. Blue Oceana wasn't so lucky and Mandy cringed as she saw The Swordfish smash into him. She didn't wait to see if Blue Oceana was okay. She waved her arms and called to Ed.

Ed threw a rope to Mandy and quickly pulled her in. He threw his arms around her as she sobbed. "You're okay, you're okay," he repeated, trying to calm her down.

"Thanks to you I'm all right." Mandy hugged Ed tightly and then pulled away from him. She hurried to the edge of the boat and searched the water for Blue Oceana.

"Do you see him?" Ed asked.

"No. Where did he go?"

Ed wrapped his arms around Mandy and hugged her. "I don't know where he is, but he'll never hurt you again. I promise you that."

Mandy had a small smile upon her face. "I'm impressed by your ability to hit Blue Oceana but not me. Blue Oceana's mother was right about you — you're a hell of a captain!"

Ed laughed. He'd never been so relieved in his entire life.

"What went wrong with him?" Mandy shuddered in fear as she thought about Blue Oceana's weird behavior.

"I'm not sure. Perhaps Mr. and Mrs. Ocean's creations weren't so perfect after all."

"Or maybe the mermen and mermaids can't handle the fact that they're different. They probably want revenge on society. But what I don't understand is why mermen would protect people from that horrid hammerhead shark."

"Have you ever heard about anyone else, other than Jacki and yourself, who survived a hammerhead shark attack while in Hawaiian water?"

"No, I haven't. Have you?"

"No. I think the mermen save women so they can turn them into mermaids."

"That's horrible!"

"Try not to think about it," Ed advised.

"Why shouldn't I? It's absolutely repulsive!"

"You don't need to think about it because I'm not like that." Ed smiled warmly at Mandy. "And hopefully you won't be looking for any other man."

"Hmm…I don't know."

"Huh?" A look of surprise and horror crossed over Ed's face.

Mandy couldn't help but laugh. "I'm just kidding." She leaned forward and kissed him.

"Let's get out of here and never come back!"

"What about Blue Oceana and the other mermen and mermaids?" Mandy asked as Ed steered the boat back towards civilization.

"Let them be. They've managed to survive for all these years in their underwater cavern. I'm sure they'll be just fine."

"I won't tell if you won't."

"I'm not telling anyone. Besides, everyone would think we were nuts!" Ed laughed.

"And there's something else we have to tell everyone," Mandy hinted.

"What?"

"We have to tell Lucy and all our friends that we're a couple now," Mandy said, smiling up at Ed.

"That's just as unbelievable as our merman story."

"Why?" Mandy began to think about the different lifestyles she and Ed lead. *Is he ashamed to be with me?*

"People would never believe I could get such a beautiful girlfriend," Ed replied, blushing slightly.

Mandy held tightly onto Ed as The Swordfish approached the dock. The setting sun made the ocean twinkle magically. Everything seemed to happen in slow motion as Ed bent down and kissed her gently.

"Thank you," Mandy muttered.

"For what?" Ed asked in a husky voice.

"For taking me on a date I'll never forget!"

* * *

One Stop Horror Shop

"Are you sure we can afford this?" Karyn asked for the hundredth time that day.

Max was hunched over the living-room table. He had a pencil hanging out the side of his mouth, a calculator in his hand and several sheets of paper in front of him. Max scribbled something down on the paper and then looked up at Karyn.

"We can't afford *not* to take Quentin's offer. Come here," Max said gently, pulling out a chair for his wife. "Do you remember the first day we met?" he asked with twinkling eyes.

"It was at Jimmy's Diner," Karyn replied, sitting down in the chair adjacent to Max. "A mutual friend had set us up."

"Do you remember why he set us up?"

Karyn smiled widely. "He set us up because he knew we had a lot in common. I know where your questions are leading, Max."

"Good. You're on the right track. Let's keep playing. Tell me what common interest you and I both shared."

"We both wanted to own a magic shop one day," Karyn said in a quiet, nostalgic voice.

"And we still do. Don't we, Karyn?"

"More than anything."

"Then we have to go for it." Lines of determination spread across Max's face. The only thing he'd ever wanted more than a magic shop was Karyn. Now that they'd been married for over two years, Max thought it was time to go after his other dream. The best part was that this other dream included Karyn as well. He knew she wanted to own a magic shop as much as he did.

"What about the mortgage we'd have to take on?" Karyn asked, biting her lip in concern. "We just paid off the mortgage on this house with the help of your parents. Won't they be upset if we get ourselves back into debt?"

"It's hardly debt. It's a business that will reap much profit. If you're really concerned about taking a loan from the bank, I can always ask my parents for help again."

"No! Your parents have already done more than enough for us. They should enjoy their money, not give it all to us."

"It's not like they don't have enough, but I know you're a proud woman. We won't ask my parents for any more money."

"I want us to make it on our own."

"If we do this, we do it our way." Max placed his hand in the air and smiled. "Scout's honor."

Karyn laughed. "You were never a Scout."

"No, but I do stand by my word. Seriously Karyn, we can do this. I know we can."

"Okay, I'm in."

"You better be. We're a team now."

"I know." Karyn kissed her husband gently on the lips. "I'd better start making dinner. Our neighbors are coming over tonight and I want to make something special."

"I'll help you, but first I'm going to call Quentin. His lawyer needs to draw up the final contract."

* * *

"I need both of your clients to sign here," Quentin's lawyer instructed Karyn and Max's lawyer.

The Shield's lawyer took the document that was offered to him. He nodded to Karyn and Max, indicating that they should sign the contract.

Karyn and Max signed the contract with great enthusiasm. They had spent many hours with their lawyer to ensure that they got the best deal possible. Now, as they dotted the "i" in their last name, they could hardly believe they were the proud new owners of Quentin's Costume and Magic Shop. All there was left to do now was change the sign above the shop's door and run the business as successfully as Quentin had.

As soon as all the papers had been signed, the lawyers shook hands. Karyn had just reached out to shake Quentin's hand when he collapsed on the floor.

"Quentin!" Max yelled in horror as he ran to the man's side.

The two lawyers quickly surrounded Quentin, making Karyn take a few steps back.

Karyn felt her heart race in fear and anticipation as she peered over their shoulders. *Quentin had been all right just a few minutes ago, so what happened?* she wondered anxiously.

"Karyn, call an ambulance."

Karyn nodded even though no one was looking at her. She quickly ran to the lawyer's desk and picked up the telephone. With shaking hands, she dialed the three numbers. Her mind was racing so fast that she couldn't concentrate on what the person on the phone was saying.

"I'll send an ambulance right away," the emergency operator said when Karyn failed to speak. "Can you tell me what the problem is?"

Karyn snapped back to reality when Max grabbed the telephone from her.

"Please send an ambulance to 21st Street North. We have an emergency here. A man in his late sixties has fallen ill."

Karyn listened as Max stopped talking.

"Yes, he's still breathing," Max replied into the telephone. "No, his pulse is fine. I have no idea what's wrong with him. He suddenly fell to the floor. He seems to be in a daze and is very cold." Max paused again. "No. His pulse is seventy beats per minute and he's breathing well."

Karyn shuddered at her husband's description of Quentin. Max made him sound like a zombie. She carefully leaned over the two concerned lawyers who were now kneeling beside Quentin. Karyn shuddered when she saw Quentin; he was lying on the floor, still breathing and his face was a healthy color. The difference between a normal person and Quentin could be seen in the eyes. Although Quentin's eyes were open, they appeared not to see anything. He looked as if he were in a completely different world.

Max held onto Karyn tightly as the paramedics took Quentin away. Quentin's lawyer also went in the ambulance, promising the others that he would keep them all informed on his client's condition.

The Shield's lawyer handed a copy of the signed contract to Karyn and Max. As they listened to the sirens disappear in the distance, the last thing on their minds were the costume and magic shop.

Karyn and Max received a call from Quentin's lawyer later that night. He told them that Quentin's condition hadn't changed. Although he seemed perfectly healthy and had good vital signs, he still refused to wake up. His glassy eyes just stared up at the doctors as if he were someplace else. Everyone at the hospital agreed that it was the creepiest thing they had ever seen.

* * *

"I think we should delay the opening of Shield's Costume and Magic Shop," Karyn said suddenly one night.

It had been three days since Quentin had fallen into his weird state. There were absolutely no changes in his condition – he still wasn't mentally present.

"What?" Max asked, sitting straight up. He'd just got into bed after three hours of planning for the opening of their shop. He was very excited about the fast approaching day and thought Karyn was too.

"It doesn't seem right. Here we are, planning the opening of our shop while poor Quentin is stuck in a hospital bed."

"Quentin will be all right," Max soothed his wife. "Maybe his body went into some sort of shock. Whatever it is, I'm sure the doctors will figure it out soon. In the meantime, we have to go on living. The world can't stop turning even though we sometimes feel like it should."

Karyn looked at Max with loving eyes. "You're right. Shield's Costume and Magic shop *will* open on September the tenth."

* * *

The process of re-organizing the store was long and tedious. Karyn took care of ordering the new supplies, while Max worked on moving the heavy objects in the store.

The sun shone through the store's large window as Karyn and Max set up a display for a book entitled Magic for Beginners, alongside an advertisement boasting it as an essential purchase for any budding magician.

"The display looks great," Max commented, while opening a large closet at the back of the room.

"The book display may look great, but that cage certainly doesn't." Karyn pointed to the cage that held a female mannequin dressed as a magician's assistant.

"It will help bring in male customers. I'll finish cleaning this old closet," Max said, changing the topic quickly. He moved a few cardboard boxes and threw them on the floor. "I'll take them to the curb for the garbage pick-up tomorrow morning...Oh gosh!"

"What's wrong?" Karyn asked breathlessly, hurrying to her husband's side. As soon as she saw what Max had, she let out a blood-curdling scream.

"Shhh..." Max moved forward to touch the disturbing object.

"Don't touch it!"

"I...I don't think it's real." Max moved closer to the skeleton that stood upright in the closet.

"It certainly looks real. Please don't touch it."

Max ignored Karyn's words and moved forward instead. His hand shook slightly as it neared the skeleton. His fingertips brushed against its cool, lifeless clavicle.

"Is it real?"

"I'm not sure, but what would a real skeleton be doing in a costume and magic shop? I'm sure it's fake."

Karyn listened to her husband's words; his voice was coming out in a hurried tone and his face was slightly pale. She wondered if he thought the skeleton was real, but was pretending it wasn't for her sake. Karyn shook her head as if to erase all the thoughts. *Of course the skeleton is fake,* she told herself.

"I have a great idea!" Karyn exclaimed suddenly. "Why don't we use the skeleton in our book display? We can dress him up as a magician and have him hold a copy of the book. What do you think, Max?"

Max stared at Karyn in surprise. "I think the display looks fine the way it is." Secretly, he had no desire to see the skeleton's face every time he went to work.

"It will look even better with Boney."

"Boney?"

"Yup," Karyn said casually as she pushed past Max and reached for the skeleton. She suppressed a shiver as her fingers grabbed the skeleton's cold neck. "Meet Boney." Karyn laughed as she made Boney wave at Max. "Help me dress him."

With little enthusiasm, Max gathered supplies and clothing for Boney's new look. He cringed as he looked at Boney's face. Underneath the costume, Boney smiled evilly. *Karyn's crazy for putting you on display,* Max said silently to Boney. *You'll scare all the customers away.*

* * *

September the tenth came very quickly. Karyn and Max were extremely busy adding the last remaining touches to their shop. Nevertheless, they still paid frequent visits to Quentin. Every time they did though, Karyn and Max were disappointed to learn that his condition hadn't improved.

"It's 9:00 AM," Karyn told Max with a wide smile.

"Time to open Shield's Costume and Magic Shop for the first time." Max motioned for Karyn to join him at the store's door. "Ready?"

Karyn nodded and then placed her hand on top of Max's. Together, they opened the store's front door to the public for the first time. The Shield's first customers came shortly after 10:00 o'clock.

"May I help you?" Karyn and Max asked at the same time.

Their two customers laughed at the dual enthusiasm. "Yes," a girl, who looked like she was in her late teens, replied. "My brother and I are starting our own magic show. We need a lot of supplies."

"A lot," the girl's brother agreed. "We're starting from scratch and will need all the basics."

"I've made a list." The girl pulled a piece of paper from her pocket and handed it to Karyn.

Karyn took the paper and read it carefully. "All right, Jodie," she began, learning the girl's name from the personalized notebook paper, "I think we have just what you need."

"That's an awfully long list," Max noted, looking over Karyn's shoulder. "May I ask how you plan to pay for it all?"

"Max!" Karyn exclaimed, appalled at her husband's poor customer service skills. "I apologize for his behavior," she added to the two teenagers.

Jodie just laughed. "That's all right. My brother, Mitchell and I are immune to that kind of treatment. We usually do the grocery shopping for our parents and are often met with such skepticism."

"Not in our shop. Now, we have the Magic for Beginners book that's on your list." Karyn quickly grabbed the book from Boney's hands and handed it to Jodie.

"Excellent," Jodie commented, flipping through a few of the pages. She handed the book to Mitchell and then headed towards the display of handcuffs. "We have to get a pair of these." She picked up the package of handcuffs and handed it to her brother.

"You can put your purchases on the check-out counter while you shop," Max offered in a friendly tone, trying to compensate for his earlier comment.

"Thank you." Mitchell gratefully placed the gathered items on the counter and then returned to his sister's side.

"You have to be more polite to our customers," Karyn whispered to Max.

"I'm sorry. I promise it won't happen again."

"It better not," Karyn muttered quietly as Jodie and Mitchell approached the counter with more items in tow. "Did you get everything you needed?"

"Yes." Jodie reached into her purse and pulled out a credit card. As she watched the surprised expression spread over Max's face, she felt like cheering. Although Jodie pretended that she didn't care what adults thought about her, it secretly bothered her. For once in her life she wanted to be treated like an equal and not a troublesome teen. Perhaps that was why she was so anxious to start a business with her brother. They wouldn't only be making money, they'd be showing the world just how mature and talented they could be.

"So, that's a magic book, handcuffs, a wand, a top hat which can hold a rabbit and fake flowers that squirt water. That's everything, right?"

"Yes." Jodie felt very powerful as the purchases were made with her credit card. *I'll show you. I'll show the world,* she thought with a smile.

* * *

"Jodie! Mitchell!" Mrs. Cartwright called as she entered their house.

"We're in the living-room!"

Both Jodie and Mitchell were sitting on the floor, surrounded by all the purchases they'd made at the Shield's Costume and Magic Shop.

Mrs. Cartwright hurried into the living-room. "I don't know whether you'll be grateful or mad when I tell you what I've done."

"What did you do?" Mitchell asked with sparkling eyes. He took much joy in hearing about other people's mishaps; as long as they weren't too serious.

"I ran into Mrs. Luther while I was at Pizza Haven..."

"Did you bring home a pizza for dinner?" Mitchell asked excitedly.

"Yes, but that's not why I need to talk to you."

"What toppings did you get?" Jodie asked with equal enthusiasm. "Did you get ham and pineapple? I hope you did. You know that Hawaiian is my favorite type of pizza."

"Pineapple has no right to be on a pizza. It makes everything soggy," Mitchell complained.

"It doesn't," Jodie objected. "If cut into small pieces, a pineapple is the perfect fruit topping for a pizza."

"Pineapples aren't fruit."

"Of course they are," Jodie retorted.

"No, they're not."

"What are they then?"

"I don't know," Mitchell grumbled in defeat.

"They're fruit. I think they grow on bushes or something."

"Enough!" Mrs. Cartwright exclaimed, raising her voice. "Stop this inane chatter right now. I swear, you two act like ten-year-olds, not the fourteen and eighteen-year-olds you are. Now, would you be quiet for a moment while I tell you where your first magic show performance will be?"

"You didn't!" Jodie exclaimed.

"Cool!" Mitchell yelled happily.

"Mom, why would you do this?" Jodie asked in exasperation. "We've just got the equipment for our magic show. We haven't practiced at all. We can't perform yet – it'll ruin our business before we even start!"

"Don't be such a worrier. It's just a small show for a group of five-year-olds. Like I was saying before I was rudely interrupted, I met Mrs. Luther in Pizza Haven. She asked how you two were doing, so I told her about your upcoming business. Then out of the blue she asked me if you'd perform at James' birthday party. Mrs. Luther said she was really desperate because the clown she'd hired had to attend court for jury duty or to stand trial or something."

"There are two things that concern me," Jodie said with raised eyebrows. "First of all, I really don't like being called upon by those who are desperate for entertainment. And second, the ambiguous way that Mrs. Luther described the absence of the clown is just plain scary."

"Okay, Mrs. Analytical," Mitchell said through a sigh. "Will you be quiet now?"

"To make a long story short, you two will be performing at James' birthday party this Sunday from 2:00 to 3:00 PM," Mrs. Cartwright explained.

"Excuse me?" Jodie cried. "Did you say Sunday? As in this Sunday? As in tomorrow?"

"Relax. We'll be ready."

"That's the attitude I like to hear, Mitchell," Mrs. Cartwright said with a smile. "Now, come and get the pizza."

Mitchell jumped up enthusiastically while Jodie followed him with much less joy.

"So, what toppings did you get on the pizza?" Mitchell asked as he sat down at the dinner table.

"Half pepperoni and half Hawaiian."

* * *

Jodie and Mitchell spent the remainder of the night and all of the next morning practicing magic tricks. They planned their routine carefully, making sure that momentum would be built throughout the performance. Jodie would start by introducing themselves as Jodie and Mitchell's Amazing Magic Show. The act would begin with Mitchell pulling a white dwarf rabbit named Fluffball from a black top-hat. Fluffball, who was graciously on loan from a neighbor, would hop around the room for a few minutes to be petted gently by the children. From there, Jodie would put handcuffs on two children and then "magically" remove them without using a key. After that, Mitchell would go around the room with a fake flower that squirts water. The grand finale would require Jodie to make Mitchell disappear into thin air with a tap of her wand.

"Hurry up," Jodie scolded Mitchell. "We have to be at Mrs. Luther's house in ten minutes."

"I'd be a lot faster if you helped me carry some of this stuff."

"I *am* carrying something." Jodie held up the small gray cage which housed Fluffball. Fluffball stared blankly while its nose moved up and down.

"Fluffball looks dumb. I wish I had a cooler rabbit to pull from the hat."

"Don't listen to that silly boy," Jodie cooed to Fluffball. "Hurry up, Mitchell." She quickened her pace.

"Why do I have to carry the majority of the stuff?"

"Because I paid for it all."

The argument between Jodie and Mitchell would've probably continued if they hadn't reached Mrs. Luther's house.

Ding Dong.

Jodie and Mitchell waited anxiously for Mrs. Luther to open the door.

Ding Dong. Ding Dong.

Jodie pressed the doorbell again. She knew this was Mrs. Luther's house, so why wasn't she replying to the ringing?

Jodie and Mitchell heard footsteps running towards them and then Mrs. Luther opened the door. Her face was flushed and beads of sweat clung to her forehead.

"I'm so glad you're here," Mrs. Luther said gratefully. "The kids really are a handful. More kids showed up than expected — half of them didn't RSVP!"

"Imagine that!" Mitchell exclaimed in fake shock. "Some people are just plain rude."

Jodie shot Mitchell an angry stare.

Mrs. Luther wasn't sure how to receive Mitchell's comment and finally decided to ignore it. "Please follow me," she instructed. "You can set up your show in the living-room. The kids are in the backyard with my husband right now."

"Thank you," Jodie said to Mrs. Luther as she led them into the nicely decorated living-room.

"You're welcome." Mrs. Luther left the living-room in a hurry.

"You have to be nicer to our clients," Jodie scolded Mitchell.

"Well, who really expects a five-year-old to RSVP?"

Jodie sighed in response. "Just help me set up."

"Is everybody ready to witness the world's best magic show?" Jodie's voice rang out loud and clear. Both she and Mitchell were dressed in long, flowing black capes. "I'd like to personally welcome you to Jodie and Mitchell's Amazing Magic Show. We have tricks that will leave you spellbound for years to come. I can assure you that your astonishment will not soon fade." Jodie smiled at the crowd of twenty-three children. She hoped her quickly thrown together introduction had impressed them. "I'd like to introduce you to Mitchell Cartwright. He's a skilled magician whose specialties include pulling a mysterious rabbit out of a top-hat. He also has a special gift that allows him to communicate with flowers. If you're good, maybe the flowers will even speak to you!" Jodie stopped talking to swallow. All the kids were playing with the spinning tops they'd received in their grab bags. Even worse was the bored expression on Mr. and Mrs. Luther's face. "Now, I present to you Mitchell Cartwright and his famous top-hat trick!" Jodie was relieved to hear a few claps as Mitchell stepped out from behind a black curtain.

Mitchell was carrying a black top-hat in one hand and a carrot in the other. "I present to you an empty hat." Mitchell talked in a deep scary voice as he showed the children the inside of the empty hat. "But with a few magic words: ally, bally, cally, dally, a rabbit will appear."

Mitchell reached into the hat and past the hidden black flap. He grabbed onto Fluffball and then gently pulled her out. Mitchell let out a startled cry; the rabbit that he was holding wasn't Fluffball.

"Mitchell! What is that thing? Where's Fluffball?"

Mr. and Mrs. Luther muttered something with a disapproving tone and stared angrily at Jodie and Mitchell. Some of the kids laughed and pointed at the pink furless rabbit, while the other kids cried.

"Um, Jodie, I think this is Fluffball."

Jodie looked at Mitchell in confusion. Then suddenly her eyes clouded over in realization. "What did you do to Fluffball?" She turned her back to the audience and lowered her voice. "Why would you shave the rabbit's fur off?"

"I didn't. I would never do that."

Jodie stared hard at her brother. "I don't believe you. I remember what you said about Fluffball – you wanted a cooler rabbit. Well, you certainly achieved that goal. Fluffball is so cold she's shivering." Jodie took the furless Fluffball from Mitchell's grasp and then put her back in the cage. "Your owner is going to kill us when she sees you," she muttered to Fluffball.

Jodie returned to the startled audience; they looked at her expectantly. Mitchell was not much support. He just stood in awe. *Mitchell knows he's in a lot of trouble,* she thought, stealing a glance at her brother.

"That was Fluffball!" Jodie announced as if the rabbit was meant to look that way. "Imagine naming a furless rabbit Fluffball! Isn't it the craziest thing you've ever heard of?"

"No. It's stupid!" a boy from the audience yelled. "What an ugly rabbit!"

"Um, time for our next trick. I'll need two volunteers from the audience." To Jodie's surprise, many kids raised their hands enthusiastically. "How about you?" She pointed to a little girl in pigtails. "And you," she added, pointing to a boy with curly brown hair. Everyone in the audience laughed as the two children approached Jodie. "What's so funny? The trick hasn't begun yet."

"Duh," the girl with pigtails said. "They're laughing because they know I hate Ronald."

"And they know I love Tammy," Ronald added, making eyes at the girl.

Tammy shuddered in response. "Let's just get this trick over with."

I don't know what Ronald sees in Tammy, Jodie thought, resisting the urge to roll her eyes at the girl. "Now, I'm going to place these handcuffs on Ronald and Tammy."

"Oh no!"

Jodie ignored Tammy's protest as she snapped the handcuffs onto Ronald and Tammy. "Now, I will magically remove the handcuffs without using a key!" She began to cover the two children's hands when the boy, who had spoken out of turn before, began to laugh. "What is it?" Jodie noticed Mr. and Mrs. Luther's disapproving gaze, but she no longer cared.

"You say 'now' a lot," the boy answered with a giggle.

"Now," Jodie said harshly, trying to annoy the boy, "I will remove the handcuffs from Ronald and Tammy."

"You already said that," a girl in the audience complained. "Would you do it already?"

Jodie gritted her teeth. "Ally, bally, cally, dally," she said with little enthusiasm. She removed the sheet from over Ronald and Tammy's hands. Jodie gasped when she saw that the handcuffs were securely in place.

"Great job," a boy said rudely, while clapping his hands mockingly.

Jodie tried to remove the handcuffs underneath the sheet once again. However, they still wouldn't come off.

"You forgot to say the magic words," a young girl in the front row told Jodie.

"I know, sweetie."

"Get these handcuffs off me right now!" Tammy demanded. "Ronald keeps looking at me. I even think he's drooling."

Jodie knew that the handcuff trick couldn't have gone worse as she ran to the magic bag to retrieve the key.

"Hurry up!" Tammy demanded as Jodie struggled with the key.

"Shit!" Jodie muttered when the key broke inside the lock.

"Jodie Cartwright!" Mrs. Luther cried in disgust. "I want to talk to you right now."

"You can't leave us like this," Tammy whined.

"Mitchell, do the flower trick!" Jodie called in desperation as she followed Mrs. Luther into the kitchen.

"Okay!" Mitchell said passionately as he retrieved the plastic flower from the magic bag. "Who wants to talk to a flower?"

"Me!" a boy at the back of the audience shouted.

"No, me!"

"Pick me!"

Mitchell laughed at the children's enthusiasm. Although Jodie's trick hadn't gone as planned, at least *he* had managed to pull that bunny from the hat. *I wonder who shaved Fluffball,* Mitchell thought.

"I want to talk to the flower," a girl with straight black hair said, standing up and running to Mitchell's side.

"Tell the flower your name."

"My name is Veronica."

Mitchell began to giggle as he pulled the lever on the flower's stem. "I tricked you," he began to say. However, he stopped speaking in mid-sentence as he watched a dark red liquid squirt all over the girl's face.

Veronica looked startled for a moment and then she began to scream. "I'm covered in blood!"

Mr. Luther ran towards Veronica and began to wipe the blood off with his shirt.

Mitchell shook harshly as he saw the blood drip down Veronica's chin. "I filled the flower with water. I know I did. So, who the hell replaced it with blood?"

Mrs. Luther had hardly begun to lecture Jodie when screams filled the house. Fearing the worst, Jodie ran quickly back into the living-room. Mrs. Luther was right behind her. Jodie could never be prepared for what she saw next. A young girl's face and Mr. Luther's chest was covered in blood.

"What did you do?" Jodie yelled in sheer horror.

"I...I did nothing."

"Then why are people bleeding?"

"They're not bleeding. I squirted blood on them from the plastic flower."

"What?" Jodie cried in disbelief. "Why would you do that?"

"I put water in the flower's stem just minutes before we left our house. The water somehow turned into blood."

"Water doesn't just turn into blood! I can't believe you're doing this, Mitchell. Nevertheless, I'm not going to let you ruin *my* magic show. I'm going to do my last trick."

"I think you two should leave," Mrs. Luther said firmly.

"No," Jodie begged. "Please, I didn't mean for any of this to happen. Let me do one more trick."

"I don't think that's a good idea..."

Jodie ignored Mrs. Luther as she grabbed Mitchell and started the last magic act.

"I saved the best trick for last!" Jodie yelled over Veronica's crying fit. "I will make Mitchell disappear!" Jodie grabbed the black wand from the magic bag and then pointed it at Mitchell who had taken his place behind the curtain. "Ally, bally, cally, dally! Make Mitchell vanish into thin air!" She pulled the black curtain away and then sighed. He was still standing there. "Why didn't you hide like we practiced?"

Many children groaned at the disappointment of learning that the trick was a fraud.

"I - can't - move," Mitchell muttered quietly and slowly.

"Stop being such a jerk." Jodie pushed her brother hard, expecting him to fall over. Instead, he stood frozen in place. "What's going on?" Jodie touched her brother's arm and then shuddered. He felt cold and hard, like a stone.

"I - - can't - - move." Mitchell's words were harder to understand this time. It looked like his lips were beginning to freeze as well.

Kids were screaming and crying as they watched Jodie frantically shake Mitchell. Mr. and Mrs. Luther were yelling at Jodie and Mitchell; they still thought this was all a joke. Jodie began to join in on the screaming when she saw Mitchell's body become transparent. She felt as if she was going to faint as she watched her transparent brother disappear into thin air.

Jodie's heart raced rapidly as she ran from the Luther's house. Frightened, she was sure that the items she'd bought from the magic shop were causing the ruckus. She knew Mitchell couldn't make himself disappear. That was the work of a supernatural, and perhaps evil, entity.

* * *

"It's six o'clock," Karyn said through a sigh. "It's time to close the shop."

Max sighed louder than Karyn had. He made no attempt to move from the chair he was sitting in.

"What's wrong?"

"You know what's wrong," Max snapped. As soon as the words, and the harsh tone in which they were spoken, left his mouth, he regretted it. "I'm sorry. I'm just so frustrated with the way things are going at the shop. We haven't sold anything since the aspiring magicians' purchases."

"I suppose you're referring to Jodie and Mitchell?"

"You know I am. I just don't understand it. Quentin's book of sales was so good."

"A bit too good, perhaps?"

Max looked at his wife with wide eyes. "You don't think he faked the records of sales in his bookkeeping, do you?"

"I don't know what to think. Maybe we were listening to our hearts rather than our heads when we bought this place. We need to admit to ourselves that costumes and magic sets are not in high demand."

"Then why did we buy the shop?"

"Because it has always been our dream," Karyn explained. "If we didn't try, we would never have known what could've been."

"You sound like you're giving up," Max pointed out anxiously. "Please don't give up — not yet anyway. Halloween is just a few weeks away. Business will be booming then!"

"I'm not giving up yet. I'm just saying that we need to be realistic. If business doesn't start to pick up soon, we'll have to think about selling this place."

"I know that you're right, but in the meantime I'm going to bombard our city with advertisements for Shield's Costume and Magic Shop. I'm also going to see Quentin. I don't care if he's still in some weird trance. He'll wake up after I'm through with him."

"You're evil," Karyn commented with a naughty laugh. "Let's close the shop now and get some dinner. I'm famished. How does a deluxe pizza from Pizza Haven sound?"

"Perfect." Max walked towards the store's door, planning to lock it so he and Karyn could leave by the back door. Before he had a chance to put the key into the lock, a person came barging through the door. Max stumbled backwards and almost fell to the floor.

"Jodie!" Karyn exclaimed. "What happened?" She could tell by the look of horror on Jodie's face that something was terribly wrong.

"It's the magic tricks you sold me," Jodie hurried to explain in between deep gasps of air. She had run the two miles it took to get to Shield's Costume and Magic Shop. Now, Jodie was experiencing a sharp pain in the left side of her stomach. She was also having a hard time catching her breath. Jodie knew that her shallow breathing was due to more than exertion; it was also caused by fear.

"The magic tricks?" Max asked in surprise. "Then I guess the book we sold you was all right." He laughed at his insensitive joke. "We don't offer refunds."

Karyn cast an angry look at Max and then turned her attention back to Jodie. Although he thought Jodie's behavior was a joke, she certainly didn't.

"Take a few deep breaths," Karyn instructed Jodie, "and then tell us everything that happened with the tricks we sold you."

Jodie took Karyn's advice and breathed deeply until she was ready to talk. "Mitchell and I used the tricks we bought from your shop for James Luther's fifth birthday party, but nothing went as planned. Mitchell pulled out a hairless rabbit from the top-hat, the handcuffs wouldn't come off the two kids who were attached to them, the fake flower squirted blood from its stem, and then the black wand made my brother disappear into thin air. You have to help me get my brother back!"

Karyn and Max looked at each other. They instinctively knew that this *wasn't* a joke.

"We don't know what's happening," Karyn finally spoke, "but we'll help you in any way we can."

"I think we better start at the scene of the crime," Max suggested. "Can you take us to the Luther's house?"

Jodie nodded. "This way."

Karyn began to follow Jodie and Max. However, she was stopped when a pair of hands grasped her shoulders. She gasped loudly, unaware that someone else was in the shop. She turned her head to see who was touching her and then screamed in horror.

Karyn's screams reached Max and Jodie, who were already well on their way out the door. Max didn't hesitate in turning around; he knew that Karyn was in danger and desperately needed his help.

Although the adrenaline that ran through Max's body had already started the fight or flight response, there was no way to be prepared for what he saw in their costume and magic shop. Max's eyes fell upon a familiar-looking skeleton dressed like a magician. He watched in horror as Boney pushed Karyn into the cage that once housed the scantly clad magician's assistant. Max shook furiously as Boney locked Karyn into the cage. *This can't be happening*, Max repeated to himself. *Skeletons can't come to life and terrorize people*. As he contemplated his next move, Jodie screamed.

Suddenly, Boney turned around in sharp, jagged movements and then stared at Max and Jodie with hollow eye-sockets.

Jodie let out another scream as Boney advanced towards them with outstretched arms. "What...what is that thing?"

"That's Boney," Max replied with a gulp.

Jodie immediately ran out of the shop.

Max wished he could follow Jodie's movements and escape from the horrible creature that was still advancing towards him. However, his feet wouldn't move out of fear and his heart wouldn't move out of love. Max knew he had to get Karyn out of that cage. His eyes traveled to Karyn; he shuddered when he realized that the bowtie, which Boney had once worn, was now tied around Karyn's mouth.

"Go...go away," Max said in a feeble voice. He watched in fear as Boney's mouth twisted into a horrible expression of pain and anger.

"I will not leave until I've taken my revenge," Boney said in a shrill voice.

Max covered his ears. The skeleton's voice was high-pitched and terribly unpleasing.

"I want my revenge!"

"Revenge for what?" Max cried, trying discreetly to move closer to Karyn. "I've never harmed you. I admit that we put you on display, but it was fun, no?" His voice came out in a pitch that could almost match Boney's; he was very nervous and in shock over finding himself communicating with a walking, talking skeleton.

"It is not you whom I seek my vengeance on," Boney replied in the same harsh tone. "It is that horrible Quentin. My spirit will not rest until I have punished him for taking my life!"

"He killed you?"

"Yes. It happened forty-five years ago in this very shop. I was only fifteen years old at the time of my death. You see, I fled from my hometown after it was struck by an awful plague. The plague killed my parents. I didn't give it a chance to get me. I made it to this town a few days later. I kept a low profile, lying about my origin to anyone whose presence I could not avoid. I had lost everything to that damn plague. Everything except my money. I had two hundred and seventy-six dollars in my pocket. With this money I tried to make a real living for myself. This opportunity came to me in the form of Quentin. I became well acquainted with Quentin by being a lodger in his two-story house. I even came to admire and respect him. Quentin quickly became like a father to me — a replacement for my recent loss. Therefore, I didn't hesitate to say yes when he proposed that we go into business together."

Max gulped and stepped backwards. He glanced at Karyn, wondering how she was doing. To his surprise, Karyn seemed to be calm and very engrossed in Boney's story. Boney was also very preoccupied with his story and thoughts. He didn't even notice the extra distance that Max had placed in between them.

"I wish I had refused Quentin's proposition," Boney continued with passion. "But no, I foolishly opened a costume and magic shop with him. The remainder of my money went to purchase the store and the supplies it would carry. Our business did very well the first few months it was opened. Much of our profit came from the theater hall which had newly opened. I suppose it was inevitable that Quentin and I would quarrel. However, one night Quentin took our argument to the next level. He tied me up and buried me alive. Although my flesh died, I did not. My spirit haunted this shop and cursed all its merchandise. The costume and magic shop, fully under Quentin's management at this point, began to fail when horrible things happened with the items purchased by the theater hall and individuals. When Quentin realized that I was causing these problems, he dug me up and locked me in that closet." Boney pointed to the closet where Karyn and Max had found him. "I stayed there until you and your wife set me free."

Max looked back and forth in between Karyn and Boney. "What do you want with us?"

"Your knowledge and your lack of interference," Boney replied simply. "I want you to tell me where Quentin is."

"Let Karyn go first, and then I'll tell you where Quentin is."

Karyn looked on as the amazing scene unfolded in front of her eyes. Although she was fascinated, she desperately wanted out of the cage.

"No," Boney said sharply, making Karyn's heart sink in despair. "I do not know if I can trust you. You must tell me where Quentin is first."

"How can I trust you? How do I know that you won't take my information and then lock me in the cage as well?"

Boney turned his head slowly to the cage which held Karyn. "That cage could hardly fit you both."

"That's what I'm afraid of," Max muttered.

"Tell me where he is."

Max looked at Boney with great fear. *If I tell this walking skeleton where Quentin is, he'll kill him,* he thought in a hurry. *I couldn't possibly live with that amount of guilt. But what if I don't tell Boney what he wants to know? Would he hurt Karyn as a punishment?* Max's head was filled with so many questions and concerns that he could no longer think straight. He was so absorbed in his thoughts that it felt unnatural when Boney wrapped his thin cold arms around him.

"Let me go," Max protested as Boney dragged him towards the cage. He was surprised at the supernatural strength the skeleton possessed.

Boney didn't say anything as he quickly unlatched the cage and threw Max in. There was so little room in the cage that Max was unable to give Karyn a comforting hug. After a few failed attempts to maneuver his hands in the tight space, he finally man-managed to remove the bowtie from around her mouth.

"Are you okay?" Max asked in concern, while looking at the dark red lines which the bowtie had produced around her mouth.

Karyn didn't reply to Max's question. "Quentin is already very ill," she spoke to Boney instead. "He's gone into some weird trance-like state. He's been like this for weeks. No one knows what the problem is."

"I put a curse on Quentin – a curse that would never allow him to sell this shop. I wanted him to feel the guilt of what he did forever."

"And if Quentin sold the shop?"

"He'd perish."

"Your curse wasn't completely successful," Karyn said. "Although Quentin's mind has stopped functioning properly, his body is still very much alive."

"Then tell me where he is so I can complete the curse."

"You can't repay violence for violence," Karyn scolded.

"Of course I can," Boney seethed.

"But you're already dead and Quentin is in some type of coma. Haven't you all suffered enough?"

"No! I must take my vengeance. If you won't help me, I'll kill you both."

"He's at Center Hospital!" Max shouted suddenly, unable to bear the thought of harm coming to either Karyn or himself.

Boney's horrible exposed jaw formed an evil smile. "I know where that hospital is."

"You won't be able to enter the hospital looking like that," Karyn tried to point out calmly. However, her heart was racing furiously.

Boney looked down at his body in a quizzical manner. "I suppose you're right." He moved his head around the room until he spotted a rack with many costumes on it. Karyn and Max watched in silence as Boney hurried over to the rack and pulled a light green doctor's outfit from it.

"Oh no," Karyn muttered as she realized what Boney was planning to do.

Boney quickly put on the doctor's outfit and then ran out the door. He didn't respond or even hesitate when Karyn and Max protested.

"What are we going to do now?"

"I don't know," Max replied somewhat restlessly. He shifted uncomfortably in the small space, grunting as he tried to move forwards. Max's hands slipped through the cage's bars and fumbled with the lock. "I can't open it." Max placed his hands clumsily on top of Karyn's. "It will be all right."

"I suppose we'll be all right," Karyn agreed, trying to sound confident. "But will we ever be able to look at this world with normal eyes again? We've seen too much."

Max cast Karyn a determined look. "We'll make it through this. I promise you that everything will be okay."

"You can't keep a promise like that."

"No, but I'll try my hardest to protect you." Max moved closer to his wife and then kissed her awkwardly. He felt his leg push painfully against the bars, but he didn't care.

"You've been trapped in a cage by a living skeleton, yet you still feel like making-out? Boy, you guys must *really* be in love."

Karyn and Max split apart as soon as they heard the voice. Both of them banged their head on the cage's bars before seeing Jodie.

"I'm so glad you're here," Max said gratefully.

"Get the key from the desk," Karyn instructed as she did her best to gesture towards the check-out desk.

"I'm so sorry for running off like that," Jodie apologized as she searched through the desk drawer. "I was so scared when I saw that skeleton. I came to my senses after ten minutes of running. After all, I've seen my brother disappear into thin air. A talking skeleton doesn't seem so weird now."

"You're forgiven, but if you really want to make it up to us you could find that damn key and get us out of here."

"Try to calm down," Max instructed Karyn. "Getting hysterical won't help the situation."

"Hysterical! Who's hysterical?"

Max stared at Karyn as her face grew red and her breathing became faster. *She's not handling this situation too well.* He prayed that Jodie would hurry up and find the key.

"I got it!"

"Thank you," Max whispered quietly, while looking up at the ceiling as he spoke.

"Open the door," Karyn demanded.

"Thanks," Jodie said sarcastically as she opened the lock. "It never crossed my mind to let you guys out."

Max let Karyn exit the cage first. Once they were both out of the cage, he said what he knew was inevitable. "Boney is going to kill Quentin. We have to stop him." Max rushed to the costume rack and then threw on a doctor's outfit. "I'll go to Center Hospital and stop Boney." Max was surprised to see two pairs of hands reach for a doctor's outfit of their own. "What are you doing?" It had never occurred to Max to take Karyn and Jodie with him. He didn't know how bad things were going to get and he definitely didn't want either Karyn or Jodie to see anything disturbing.

"We're coming with you," Karyn said in a determined voice, the one that Max had fallen in love with.

"Fine. Let's go."

The sun was beginning to set as the threesome raced to the Shield's car. They arrived at the hospital ten minutes later. Karyn, Max and Jodie were sure they'd beaten Boney to the hospital. At least they thought they had. Their minds were quickly changed when they spotted Boney entering the hospital through a back door.

"How did he get here before us?" Jodie whispered.

"I'm not sure," Max admitted. "But the important thing is that we follow him and stop him from killing Quentin."

"Then we figure out a way to get my brother back, right?"

Karyn nodded. "Of course."

"Let's go." Max hurried towards the door in which Boney had entered the hospital. He looked expectantly at Karyn and Jodie when they failed to follow him. "What's wrong? Why aren't you coming? We have to find Boney and Quentin now."

"Um, Max, I think we've already found them."

Max followed the direction which Karyn's finger was pointing. He gasped when he saw Boney in a patient's room.

Max tore his eyes away from the window and ran into the hospital. Karyn and Jodie were right behind him as he hurried through the hall and towards the occupied room. Before Max could open the door Boney came charging out of the room. Boney collided with Max, causing them both to fall into a heap on the floor.

"How did you get here?" Boney snarled. However, he didn't wait for an answer as he quickly got to his feet and continued down the hall.

Karyn ran into the room Boney had just exited. "No one was in here. It looks like this room hasn't been used for awhile."

Max scarcely heard Karyn's words as he stared at the bone which lay on the floor in front of him. He picked up the bone and turned his head to see Boney turn a corner of the hall. Max realized, after the fall, that a limp now accompanied Boney's jagged movements. Suddenly, a brilliant idea popped into Max's head.

"We have to follow him," Max urged.

Karyn and Jodie raced by Max's side as he turned the corner of the hall. They all spotted Boney as he went into another room.

"I remember that room," Karyn said breathlessly. "That's the room where I visited Quentin. Oh my gosh, he's found Quentin!"

One after the other, Karyn, Max and Jodie rushed into the hospital room. They all gasped in unison when they saw Boney standing over a single bed which contained an unconscious Quentin.

The threesome's gasps alerted Boney of their presence. In response, Boney hissed and threw his skinny arms in the air. He hoped to scare the unwelcome guests away so that he could continue with his plan to eliminate Quentin.

As Karyn let out a startled cry, and Jodie hid behind her, whimpering softly, Max knew he was going to be the only one to stand his ground. He challenged Boney by staring into his eye sockets. Boney cast an evil look at Max, grabbed Quentin's neck and then began to squeeze.

"Please stop," Karyn begged Boney.

"Where's the hospital staff when you need them?" Jodie cried unhappily.

Max said nothing as he reached for the large chrome metal pole which held an IV. He moved swiftly as he lifted the pole high in the air and swung it against Boney's body.

When the pole hit Boney, his skeletal body shattered into a hundred pieces. Each bone disjointed itself from the other and fell to the floor with a loud clatter.

Jodie covered her ears and closed her eyes while Karyn looked at the pile of bones in amazement. Max's eyes were nowhere near the floor; he was too busy looking at Quentin.

Quentin began to stir and then suddenly his eyes flew open. He coughed weakly and slowly lifted his arms to his neck, rubbing his hands over the red marks that Boney's fingers had produced. "What am I doing in a hospital bed?" he asked feebly.

"Quentin!" Karyn exclaimed. "You're all right."

"Why wouldn't I be?" Quentin said in an almost mocking tone as he sat up. "Now, would someone tell me what's going on here?" His voice trailed off as he looked upon the broken skeleton on the floor. He suddenly looked very guilty. "That heap of bones isn't just a broken hospital display, is it?"

Max shook his head furiously. "So, it's true. Everything that Boney told us about the partnership and murder was true."

"Boney?"

"That's what I called the skeleton Max and I found in the closet," Karyn explained. "I thought it was just a plastic skeleton."

"Karyn was wrong," Jodie said angrily, looking at Quentin through slit eyes. "And because of you my brother has disappeared. Bring him back now!"

"Hold on a minute," Quentin said, while raising his hands in the air. "I don't know what any of you are talking about."

"Yes, you do," Max argued. "You killed your business partner and then hid his bones in a closet."

"What I don't understand," Karyn began slowly, "is why you'd put your life in danger by selling the store. You realized the power of Boney's curse, didn't you?"

Quentin nodded sadly. "I understood perfectly well, but it doesn't matter any more. After I was diagnosed with lung cancer, I decided to sell the shop. By either the power of Boney's curse or the failure of my lungs, I knew I was a goner." Quentin stopped talking and chuckled to himself like a madman. "You know what's ironic? A large portion of the money made from my business was spent on cigars." He laughed again, this time in a much sadder tone.

"You're a liar, cheat and murderer!" Max yelled furiously. "No one feels sorry for you."

"It doesn't matter," Quentin replied in a melancholy voice. "I have enough pity for the both of us."

"You should feel pity for us!" Karyn shouted. "We're stuck with a failing business because of you."

"No we're not," Max said. "Quentin is going to buy the shop from us for the exact price we paid for it."

"I will not!" Quentin protested, getting onto his feet.

"Oh yes you will."

"No way."

"If you refuse to pay us what we deserve, we'll tell the police about the murder you committed forty-five years ago."

"You have no incriminating evidence to prove my guilt. The police would never believe you."

"Do you really want to take that chance, Quentin?" Max sneered.

"Fine. I'll buy the shop back for the amount that you paid."

"I'm glad that everything has worked out for Karyn and Max," Jodie interjected with frustration. "But what about my brother? He's still missing."

Max had just opened his mouth to speak when a ringing cut him off.

Jodie grabbed the ringing cell phone from her pocket and quickly answered it. "Hello? Oh my gosh! Mitchell! Are you okay? Are you visible?"

Karyn couldn't help but smile as she watched Jodie speak to her brother. By the sound of her voice, she was sure that Mitchell was back to his normal self.

"Can I borrow your cell phone?" Max asked as soon as Jodie had finished talking to her brother. "Quentin has to make a call to his lawyer. A new contract for the purchase of Shield's Costume and Magic Shop has to be written up immediately."

* * *

The sale of Shield's Costume and Magic Shop went through two weeks after the incident at the hospital. Although Max was usually one to keep his word, he was unable to do so in this case; he told the police that Quentin had confessed to murdering a man forty-five years ago. A warrant for Quentin's arrest was issued shortly after the police had been informed about his misconduct. Regardless, it was too late. Quentin had died in his home the night before.

Jodie and Mitchell Cartwright had a lot of apologizing to do for the magic show they had put on at the Luther's house. They blamed the incident on the malfunction of the tricks they had bought. Rumors about Jodie and Mitchell's amazing magic show circulated around their whole town, causing them to get many offers to put on a *horror* show. With the right equipment bought from a large chain store, Jodie and Mitchell successfully adapted their business, put on many horror shows, and flourished financially.

As for Karyn and Max, they moved from their sleepy town to the city a few months later. They had a store constructed from scratch and then filled it with homemade magic tricks and costumes. The terrifying skull which lay on the check-out desk was a customer favorite. Shield's Homemade Costume and Magic Shop went on to become a big hit, and soon, a chain developed, opening many stores across the country. It was so successful, in fact, that maybe you've even seen one in your own neighborhood.

* * *

About the Author

Heather Beck is a Canadian author and screenwriter who began writing professionally at the age of sixteen. Her first book was published when she was only nineteen years old. Since then she has written several well-reviewed books.

Heather recently received an Honors Bachelor of Arts from university where she specialized in English and studied an array of disciplines. Currently, she is working on two young adult novels and has six anthologies slated for publication. As a screenwriter, Heather has multiple television shows and movies in development. Her first short film, *Young Eyes*, premiered in 2009.

Besides writing, Heather's greatest passion is the outdoors. She is an award-winning fisherwoman and a regular hiker. Her hobbies include swimming, playing badminton and volunteering with non-profit organizations.